# Ganga's Choice

## and Other Stories



**VAASANTHI**

*Translated from the Tamil original*

THORNBIRD

NIYOGI BOOKS

Published by
NIYOGI BOOKS
Block D, Building No. 77,
Okhla Industrial Area, Phase-I,
New Delhi-110 020, INDIA
Tel: 91-11-26816301, 26818960
Email: niyogibooks@gmail.com
Website: www.niyogibooksindia.com



Editor: K.E. Priyamvada
Design: Shashi Bhushan Prasad
Cover design: Akankshya Padhi

ISBN: 978-93-91125-43-1
Publication: 2021



Printed at: Niyogi Offset Pvt. Ltd., New Delhi, India

*To Vikram, my grandson,*
*who, when five years old,*
*asked a profound question,*
*'Are we real?'*
*I told him,*
*'We are. Because we feel.'*

# Contents

# The Testimony

Mother was taking a long time to lock the door. The girl stood mute and inert, not attempting to ponder why this simple act would need so much time.

She opened her handbag and checked its contents once again. The brownish yellow paper was there. Someone pulled her dupatta. Startled, she turned. Her little brother, Chinna Thambi, was looking at her with panicked eyes. 'I do not feel like accompanying you. Both of you can go.'

'Why are you making such a fuss?' she asked, slightly frustrated. 'Behave responsibly. You are the only male in this house,' she said, patting his bony little shoulder.

'What is Thambi saying?' asked mother.

She lost her cool. 'Nothing! It is getting late amma! Why on earth are you taking so long to lock the door?'

'I am not able to lock the door, dear.'

Amma's fingers quivered. She could not insert the key in the keyhole with her quaking hand.

'Give it to me. I will lock the door,' the girl said, taking the lock and key from her mother.

A few heads peeked out of houses nearby. Some neighbours emerged from their houses. Amma covered her head with her sari, almost hiding her face.

The girl held Chinna Thambi's chilled hands and stepped out. An eerie silence seemed to smother the entire street. Stray dogs lifted their heads and looked down again, without barking. Birds flew by noiselessly. Even noise from vehicles seemed absent. The fixed stares increased her apprehension. Her legs seemed to buckle under her. She felt like touching her mother's sari and muttering, 'I do not feel like accompanying you. Both of you can go'. It seemed like the whole street, including the strays, were frozen as they moved forward on weak legs. She expected someone to come forward, like in the movies, and boost their morale by saying, 'You need not go. We will take care'.

'So, you are off?' asked the lady next door, in much the same tone as one might ask, 'Is the body ready for burial?' Coming nearer, she added, 'They say you must speak cautiously'.

The girl turned and spied the lady's husband at the window. She felt buried in his glare which conveyed a thousand cautions. He had repeated the same words when he happened to see her, without his wife's urging, 'They say you must speak cautiously'.

She did not need to ask who 'they' were, who said this. She was familiar with every frozen person's voice in this street and the next. They were the ones who had hailed her as a loving mate, one of their own, endearingly. Today, they believed their fate rested on her testimony. She felt unable to breathe when she felt their collective voices and fears crawl and climb rapidly onto her back. Even Amma and Chinna Thambi joined them, weighing her down. She felt weary, as if her back had broken.

For some reason, mother hesitated and stood still.

'Amma, get moving! Do not respond to anyone now!'

Amma followed her in silence. Chinna Thambi walked with her, gripping her hand tightly. They saw the old man who lived in the house at the farthest end of the street. He was sitting in front of the small corner shop and smoking a beedi. It would be hard to avoid him, she thought. He had been visiting them every night for the past 10 days to pontificate, including last night.

'Those who are gone, are gone forever. Can we bring them back? You should concern yourself with those who are alive,' he had said.

The girl wondered how he could talk to them that way, sitting inside the smoke-blackened walls. Amma sat in silence, staring at the wall. She then buried her head in her knees. Her back shook with her sobs.

'You will act with prudence if you consider the wellbeing of your neighbours, relatives and dear ones, our community.'

The girl controlled the waves of emotion rising inside her because there was no need to respond to this old man.

'What's the point of my standing here and talking if you don't respond?'

She erupted suddenly. 'Grandpa, what would you have done if you had experienced what we have gone through?

What would be your thinking? Would you have let bygones be bygones?'

He was mildly shocked as he faced this question from a young girl, her eyes wide and chest heaving. He shook his head repeatedly as fear gripped the pit of his stomach. He trembled. He left the house in silence. He said something almost under his breath as he was leaving. She remembered the panic, helplessness and anger in his eyes.

'Your quest for justice might endanger all of us. It might endanger those left of your family.' He took courage in her silence and continued. 'If you point out the ones who did it, will their hands be plucking flowers?'

'Grandpa, please leave.'

'Leave!' she shouted when the silly old man opened his mouth again.

She spat on the ground in disgust and cussed him for a long time after he left. She buried her head in Amma's lap and cried hard when she remembered the helplessness and fear in his eyes. She could almost see the ash-white look of fear in Grandpa's eyes. There was panic coupled with that fear.

She now walked with her head bowed. She was afraid that he would attempt to talk to her. It was easy to be unyielding within four walls. Weakness engulfed her as she walked along the street. She felt she could trip on a blade of grass. Sighting any police person brought on panic attacks. Her tongue had refused to cooperate when they had questioned her. She had no idea what going to the court entailed. She had never stepped into one before. She had no clue about who would defend her.

She could not understand when the lady next door asked, 'Won't you have a government lawyer to defend you?'

She was not aware of it. 'I guess I will have to talk for myself,' she had responded.

She had received an inscrutable and strange glance in response. 'You are a young girl. What can you do alone?'

She had felt angry. 'Ask your husband to accompany me!'

Her neighbour stopped talking after that. However, the news that the girl had received a summons from the court spread like wildfire and impelled everyone to come to her house. She had already been disconcerted after receiving that brownish yellow paper summoning her to court. Now, everyone held forth. They preached. They warned. They blamed her for speaking to the police. They declared that there was no justice for those who were wronged. Their speeches had frightened her more than that piece of paper.

She sensed someone walking with her and turned.

The old man spoke quickly, as if afraid she would escape him. 'It seems that rascal has some big plan. He has sworn to finish us all off if you speak against him. The police and government are on his side. Think well and make a decision!' He went back and sat on the bench without waiting for her response.

She could have given a whiplash had he stood a minute longer, she thought. 'All of you can go to hell. You have not understood my grief. Who cares if you are alive or dead? I need justice. I am not a thinking human if I do not accuse the guilty person. Why else do we have courts and testimonies?'

She was unable to contain the waves of resentment rising within her. She walked on, breathing heavily. Her eyes misted and her face reddened. She realized that Amma and Chinna Thambi had become deeply discouraged after Grandpa's speech.

'Amma, come on! That oldie can only talk like that—impotent bastards! Have you too forgotten what you witnessed? Has your anger dissipated?' Amma walked on, afraid to even respond. There was no bus or autorickshaw because of the curfew. They had to walk four kilometres to reach the court. They were all tired and sweating hard half-way through. They had been unable to eat breakfast that morning. Even Chinna Thambi had been unable to eat. They had each drunk a cup of tea and that was all. She became alert when Chinna Thambi tightened his grip on her hand and slowly turned. Ten or 15 middle-aged men were following them. They had pulled their *veshtis*[1] tight between their legs, as if readying for a serious fight. They might have been part of the mob the other day, she thought. 'Why are you following us?' she wanted to ask, but decided against it. Instead, she turned away and walked on in silence. Her tongue had curled into itself. 'Why am I afraid when I should be angry?' she questioned herself.

---

1 *Veshti:* a length of cloth that is wrapped around the waist and tucked in at the waistline. This garment is chiefly worn by men in south India.

'Hey little boy!' a man hailed them, as if talking to Chinna Thambi. 'Tell this to your sister: she should not increase her enemies if she wants to live in peace.'

Chinna Thambi looked at her. Her face reddened and she walked swiftly.

'Tell her to think well and speak,' said another man. 'Otherwise, things might take a turn for the worse.'

She felt like strangling all of them. Chinna Thambi started crying quietly.

'No, no! Stop crying and wipe your eyes,' she scolded him under her breath.

The crowd followed, heckling them. Her legs felt like rubber even before they reached the court. Her heart felt heavy, with the sound of an axe resonating within. Her throat felt dry. She realized that Amma and Chinna Thambi had frozen for an entirely different reason. Kishorilal stood before her. He seemed to tower over her, covering heaven and earth, making it impossible for her to move forward.

'You have thought about what you want to say, haven't you?' he asked in a low voice. 'Do you know what will happen if you speak against us? You will cease to exist. The police have been bought. All witnesses are on our side now. Even your government lawyer has come over to our side.'

She felt hatred well within her and searched for the appropriate words to abuse him with.

Kishorilal looked at Amma and Chinna Thambi with narrowed eyes. 'Pray that at least these two will live,' he told her.

There were numerous black coats hovering in front of the court. The summons said she had to present herself in the court at 11 a.m.

'Time to go to court. Leave way,' she said.

Kishorilal moved aside. 'Remember,' he said.

A black coat approached her and said, 'Come on, come on. They are waiting for you.'

Amma and Chinna Thambi were asked to stand aside. The court was overflowing. She searched for relatives or acquaintances among the crowd. There were none.

'Who is the government lawyer?' she asked hesitantly.

'That's me,' said the black coat standing beside her.

She wondered how this lawyer, who had not even spoken to her until then, could possibly defend her. She remembered Kishorilal saying that this lawyer was on his side. 'Will our case win?' she asked.

The lawyer stared at something distant. 'Very hard,' he replied, shaking his head and pressing his lips together.

She felt angry. 'Why? Why will we not get justice? Will these heinous criminals not get punished? Isn't there something called the law?'

The lawyer came close and spoke in her ear. 'What can we do? The police and establishment are on their side.'

'Aren't you too on their side?' she wanted to ask but controlled herself.

'What will the poor judge do?' the lawyer lamented. It seemed like he was sorrier for the judge than for her.

The court was packed. It seemed to cast a hostile glance at her and say, 'This woman is the one who should go to prison.' Gandhi smiled a toothless smile framed on the wall behind the judge's chair.[2]

The trial commenced. Witnesses testified one after the other. Some lived in her street and had witnessed the incident. They came and stood in the witness stand. The lawyer mentioned that only 44 out of the 73 witnesses had come in.

Many insisted that they had been out of town on the day of the incident. Others said that they had only heard about it and had not witnessed it. She looked around, confused. Kishorilal, the accused, stood with his gang and thousands of other Kishorilals. The judge and Gandhi behind him had all turned into Kishorilals. Someone called her to the witness stand.

Her body moved but her soul was afloat somewhere in space.

They asked for her name, where she lived, her father's name, her mother's name, the names of the living, and the list of the dead. Total number dead, 14. Her tongue twisted when she uttered their names. She felt sick and faltered remembering their names. The court laughed. So many? In the same house? Yes. They were a large joint family, all living together. Husband, wife, and kids. Was 14 improbable? A

---

2 In India, the photograph of Mahatma Gandhi, who spearheaded India's nonviolent struggle for independence from the British, is placed behind the judge's chair in many courts of law.

man in the crowd uttered something lewd. The crowd jeered. She looked at the judge in confusion. Kishorilal was sitting in the judge's chair.

'Did you witness the incident?'

The incident. She felt dizzy just thinking about it. She had to remember and string words together to describe the incident…the murderous gang entering the house at night…how they smashed everything inside…how they set fire to the house…how they dragged her father and elder brother into the street and set fire to them…how she, Amma and Chinna Thambi escaped to the terrace in terror…what she witnessed from the terrace, weeping and devastated… how everyone in the street looked on in silence…how the three of them hid on the terrace until dawn. And how they came down and screamed in agony when they saw the 14 blackened corpses…

The judge spoke. 'Why are you not answering? At least answer this question. Are your mother and younger brother the only remaining ones in your family?'

She looked up with a start. She wondered if she would be able to provide the right answer.

'Yes, Sir.'

'Where were you when the violent incident happened?'

'On the terrace…'

'Did you witness the incident from there?'

Her stomach lurched in the dead silence of the court. Something powerful rose inside her and strangled her throat. A mix of fury, sorrow, and helplessness hit her like a raging hurricane, suppressing her nerves and very being. She could only feel air when she tried to open her mouth.

'Speak up! Did you see what happened downstairs?'

The girl bowed her head and was worried what words she would frame. They seemed to slip from her memory. 'Are your mother and young brother the only remaining ones in your family?' Who asked this and why? She felt dizzy. She opened her mouth. It seemed to speak of its own volition. Separated from her body.

'No, I did not.'

She was astonished by the stunned silence around her. She felt surprised, as if she too were an observer among the crowd watching her.

'You have informed the police that you witnessed the incident. You have also informed them that these are the accused.'

The mouth spoke: 'I lied. Please forgive me. Forgive me.'

The court erupted, making her feel breathless and almost knocking her down. She freed herself from the din and came out of the court. The government lawyer had disappeared somewhere among the crowd.

Amma and Chinna Thambi were waiting for her. She wondered what to tell them. Grief overwhelmed her. She stood, her head bent, totally defeated.

'Let's go home,' Amma said. China Thambi grasped her hand.

She could feel the sense of relief in Amma's voice and her brother's touch.

She wanted to beat her breasts and wail, ignoring the fact that she was in a public street.

Original Tamil title: *Vaakkumoolam*
Translated by: Sukanya Venkataraman
First published in *Guftugu*, September 2020, https://guftugu.in/2020/09/11/the-testimony-by-vaasanthi/

# The Symbol

It seemed as if someone was standing on the landing. It also seemed no one was there. The sun had never managed to penetrate the landing, which stood beyond the four front steps and the small corridor. Not since this house was built. One needed to carry a lamp to see a visitor's face. At least until the house was electrified. A small chimney lamp used to burn constantly in the pooja room for this purpose. One could only see a person's face after they had moved into the courtyard beyond the landing. Now, it seemed someone was definitely standing on the landing.

Soundari Ammal's back remained curved in her easy chair as she lifted her head and asked, 'Who is that?'

No one visited unannounced. Definitely not strangers. They needed a certain standing to even step into Soundari Ammal's house. Who might this be? Could it be Chellappa? If so, why was he standing on the landing? He would have taken off his slippers and quickly entered the house. Soundari Ammal covered her shoulder with her sari with some difficulty. She wore no blouse. It was getting extremely hard to insert her hand into a blouse. Anyway, hadn't the blouse only been introduced recently? If someone came to visit from Chennai, she would ask Sabapathy's wife Karpagam or their daughter Mallika to help her wear a blouse. Now it seemed like someone was standing on the landing. What could she do if someone visited out of the blue?

'Hey Karpagam…Mallika…it looks like someone is standing on the landing.' The words were soundless. Soundari Ammal felt a mild panic. Why wasn't she able to use her voice? Mallika, Karpagam, Sabapathy. The words rose from the pit of her stomach and were buried in her heart. The clear bronze-like voice. The bell-like voice. The exceptional voice. What had happened to her much-acclaimed voice? Soundari Ammal struggled to say the words again and again. She could not utter a sound.

Someone on the landing…suddenly, she knew. Light spread in a circle, as if a curtain were lifting. Ah, our Dhanam. In her Benaras silk sari and traditional nose ring—her feet together, her hands outstretched, her face expressive.

'*Varugalaamo*?'….May I come, to sing and dance? The song combined with tiny cymbals resonated and flooded her. Soundari Ammal melted. Her eyes filled and her head and hands moved in rhythm to the song. The song flooded from inside her and poured out.

> *'May I come to stand beside you,*
> *To celebrate, sing and dance*
> *May I?'*

She forgot herself. Was there any holy sanctum higher than this? Dance, Dhanam, dance. How many years has it been since I saw you dance? When she looked up after wiping her tears, Dhanam had disappeared. There were some shadowy figures on the landing.

'We're late because the market was so crowded,' Karpagam was saying as she entered the brighter courtyard. Soundari Ammal felt like she had been hit on the head. Her heart was flooded by an inexplicable disappointment.

'Did someone come in search of me, *Akka* (elder sister)?' asked Sabapathy.

'No one came in search of you.'

'Anyone came to see you? Did Chellappa come by?'

'No, no.'

Soundari felt confused.

'What is it, Akka?'

'Nothing. I must have had a dream.'

'A dream?'

Soundari felt a slow smile spreading through her. 'Yes, it seemed so real. Who do you think came in my dream? Dhanam was in my dream in her Benares silk sari and lovely nose ring! She even danced for me. She gestured beautifully for "Can I come…?" Now that is what I call true art and dance!'

Sabapathy looked at Karpagam and laughed. 'Karpagam, bring some coffee. Why don't you bring those greens? Akka and I will clean the leaves.'

Soundari Ammal, still stunned by the apparition, stared

at the landing. It was pitch black there. Had it been a dream after all?

'Here's some coffee,' Karpagam's voice and even her placing a bunch of greens seemed dream-like to Soundari. However, it seemed that the ecstasy she had felt on seeing Dhanam's dance was real. Her stance, her gestures, her expressive eyes…ah, how could one call that a dream? The thrill she had felt was still apparent. Waves of music rose inside her, grew wings and took flight.

'May I come…oh my lord…'

'Akka, is Dhanam still standing there?'

Soundari, whose gaze was at the landing while cleaning the greens, turned her head and smiled. Sabapathy was intent on chopping the greens finely. She wanted to say something more about Dhanam's dance but contained her enthusiasm. Sabapathy's transformation amazed her. His mridangam playing when he was just eight had been stupendous. However, their father had insisted on sending him to school and killed the music in Sabapathy. A clerk's job, marriage over 40, a school teacher for a wife, prestige, respect, and other such rubbish had suddenly taken precedence. It seemed like their very blood had changed now.

'It must be 10 years since she died?'

'Who?'

'I was talking about Dhanam Akka.'

'Hmmm, even longer than that. She lived like a hermit in her older years.'

'Yes, I've heard that.'

'A man called Rangoon Sundaram was smitten by her music and dance. He showered her with gold and diamonds. Dhanam heard that he had faced terrible losses in Rangoon and was struggling for his next meal. She bundled up all the gold, diamonds and silver vessels he had given her and handed it over. It seems his wife was astonished and fell at Dhanam's feet in utter gratitude.'

'People like this too have lived.'

'Of course! Enlightenment, Sabapathy. Those with enlightened knowledge are also compassionate.'

'Have you finished cleaning and chopping the greens?' asked Karpagam, her voice rising. 'Mallika and Senthil will be coming in to eat soon.'

Soundari fell silent. This was Karpagam's gesture to indicate that she had spoken enough.

'We're done. Please take it,' said Sabapathy.

Karpagam's toe rings tinkled as she walked towards them. The thali on her neck swung to and fro as she bent to collect the greens.

'Shall I mash the greens and make a spicy brinjal *kuzhambu* (curry) Akka?' asked Karpagam in a conciliatory tone.

'Do that. Make sure Mallika and Senthil like it too.'

'I'm making a potato roast just for them.'

Soundari knew that continuing in this vein would give Karpagam peace, if not satisfaction. Why are they scared to death? They fear ghosts. They fear their own shadow. Every word from my mouth seems like a ghost from the past to them. Karpagam would have chased me into the street if I did not receive a pension. She relaxed in her chair now that the greens had been cleaned.

The walls, above the height of a man, were crammed with photographs. Soundari was in all of them with a big dot on her forehead, her lovely saris and jewels, and a wide smile. They were proof of the accolades she had received from VIPs from Thiruvidangoor to Baroda. *Sangeetha Bhushani*, *Gana Soundari*, *Gana Saraswathy*, *Kalamamani*—and so many others she could not even remember. How could she forget music, her very breath? It was nearly time for her last journey. Still, she felt a thrill in her very veins when she heard music. A Hyderabad Minister had mentioned that Sangeetham (music) and Soundari were one and the same. She could see that photo in the far-right corner. He had said the truth. These people just pocketed the pension. How could they forget? I have become a mere symbol to these callous idiots. Soundari closed her eyes exhausted.

'Switch on that radio, Sabapathy. There will be music now.'

There was only static. Then the music came.

*'Devi… you are my refuge,*
*Meenalochini who lives in Madurai'*

In a flash, all inanimate objects around Soundari ceased to exist and her thoughts stilled. She was in another world, in the presence of the divine.

*'De…viii…'*

Ah, what is this? This female singer has stopped already. How many more *sangathis*[1] she could have sung! People have stopped singing *sangathi*s these days…Perhaps it is laziness. Perhaps it is something else. Must mention this to Chellappa, she thought.

'Have you stopped the song, Sabapathy?'

'I switched it off, aunty. The song was not nice at all?' answered Senthil.

'The song was not bad, although there was no *sangathi*. You don't seem to like classical music.'

'It is not that really. A visitor is here.'

'Who?'

'Who knows? Father is entertaining the lady.'

Why is this boy always so angry?

'Come in and eat. You are always angry when you are hungry,' chided Karpagam, in a low voice.

'Who has come to visit, Sabapathy?'

'Someone from Madras. They want an interview for their magazine.'

'Who do they want to interview?'

'You.'

'Me?'

Before they could continue the conversation, Senthil rushed in again. 'There's no need to give any interview.'

She felt a moment's chill. The determination in his face and eyes reminded her of many other things. This boy is only 22, but his anger was old and known to her.

---

1 *Sangathi*: embellishment of a song in south Indian or Carnatic classical music.

When she saw a lady come inside with her hands folded respectfully, Soundari felt a connection.

'Please come in,' she said, ignoring Senthil.

Chellappa felt as if shapeless specks were flitting before his eyes. His neck ached after almost two hours of scrutinizing ancient books, with pages falling apart. There was not even a proper fan in the library. Only Chellappa could focus on his study despite the noise it made.

Enough for today. Chellappa carefully closed the book and placed it on a shelf. 'See you,' he told Santhanam, the librarian, as if he was taking leave of his family.

'It seems like I keep this library open just for you,' said Santhanam. 'People are not interested in reading. Even those who visited libraries earlier are sitting in front of their TV now.'

Chellappa attempted to leave on the pretext of spitting out the betel leaves and nut he had been chewing. Santhanam would not be able to stop once he got going. Chellappa felt uncomfortable when he heard Santhanam speak of his books as treasures that were being wasted.

'I will be happy if there are a few people more like you Chellappa,' Santhanam went on. 'Your father's dream was to see you as an educated man, an academic. Today, you are a highly respected college professor…' Chellappa felt embarrassed as he heard these words. With a quick nod and shy smile, he stepped out.

Santhanam had repeated these words innumerable times. Yet, Chellappa felt a thrill every time they were uttered. He felt uneasy because Santhanam thought to say this every time they met. He felt a slight sense of humiliation.

This unease followed Chellappa as he walked towards his house. Father had never worn a shirt or slippers when he walked these streets. He had been a strong, well-built man. Chellappa, the last child, remembered running to keep up with him.

If a servant came by from Mettu Theru Mirasu's house, father walked even faster. The *mirasu* (landlord) would be sitting on a large swing with silver fittings in the front porch of his big house, using his foot to move it to and fro. The swing would stop when father entered. Father would almost bend double in obeisance, his big body diminishing in size.

'Did you call me, *Sami*?'[2]

Seeing his father's extreme servility used to make Chellappa think that it was indeed the Sami, the very god, sitting on that swing. 'Sami' would take a betel leaf from a silver box, tear off the leaf's vein and deign to address father.

'My daughter's wedding has been finalized. There are four or five auspicious dates in the month of *thai* (mid-January to mid-February). Let me know which date works for you. You must play the *Nadhaswaram*[3] at the wedding.'

---

2 *Sami*: here it means, a respectful way of addressing an 'upper caste/class' man. Sami also could mean god.

3 *Nadhaswaram*: a traditional classical double reed wind instrument, played to the accompaniment of drums on auspicious occasions.

Appa's face would blossom as if he had received a boon. 'Where else would I play if not at our house's wedding, Sami?'

Still, the accountant present in the room would say the dates and father would choose one.

'Very good. Let us keep the wedding on that day.'

When they were leaving, the 'God' would address them, 'You must play the song *saragunapaalimpa* during the *jaanavaasam* when the groom is brought through the street to the venue.'

Appa would smile happily, showing his teeth stained with beetle juice. 'Of course, Sami.'

Appa would literally float home, smiling fondly at Chellappa now and then. From then on, he would then rehearse *saragunapaalimpa* every day. During the new groom's procession, he would seem like a king when he played *sankarabaranam* or *mohanam* in the middle of the street. At that moment, the accompanying drummers, the *mirasu* and the groom's party all seemed like father's vassals, paying obeisance to him. Chellappa would feel so proud. After the procession, father, the accompanying artists and Chellappa would sit in the stone shelter at the end of the street. Hungry and tired, he would fall asleep on his father's lap. Finally, the food would arrive in a bucket. Father would spread the cloth hung on his shoulder. A plaintain leaf with a mixture of rice, vegetables, lentil soup and other ingredients would be emptied into it. They would eat the food sitting there, dispose of the leaf in the nearby canal and clean their mouths. They would then return home, immeasurably tired.

Chellappa felt amazed when he thought back. Father had not complained even once. However, he had some firm convictions. He did not know if they were the result of something lacking in father's life or because of some longing.

It was unbearably hot. Chellappa reminded himself to buy a new umbrella. He had forgotten his old one in the library and someone had made off with it. 'You were feeling bad that no one except me visited this library. Someone else has come and stolen my umbrella,' he had told Santhanam and they had laughed. It was only in the heat that Chellappa missed his umbrella and realized that it was a symbol of prestige, something his father had never possessed.

He walked along, using a hand to shade his eyes. Thank God he had good slippers to protect his feet. They were a symbol. His shirt and the cloth over his shoulder were symbols too. Father had felt that his identity had been stripped because he had been refused these.

He saw the woman as he was crossing the North Masi Street. She appeared to be from Madras or Bombay—city bred, certainly not from this part. She wore dark glasses and had covered her head with her sari as protection against the sun. 'Excuse me,' she addressed him. 'Could you tell me where Soundari Ammal's house is?'

'Of course,' he responded.

'Turn left at the end of the street and go straight. It is the last house in that row.'

'Thank you,' she replied with a smile.

'Will she be at home?'

'Where else will she go? She's 82.'

'Thanks,' she said and started walking in the direction he indicated. He always addressed Soundari Ammal as aunt. His heart blossomed when he thought of her and he smiled even without realizing it. He felt that there was not much difference between his father and aunt.

Mandakini thought she should have brought an umbrella. She knew it would be hot in southern India, but no one had told her that it would be boiling. It seemed like there was not much difference between the seething hot Rajasthan and Tamil Nadu in high summer. The heat was blinding, bleached white. Still, just as there seemed to be a connection between sun and colour, there seemed to be a link with art, music, sound and rhythm. Just like the link between, lust, love, rage, and humiliation...

The streets seemed to have wrapped up all the colour and verve she had imagined, cloaked in a shroud of silence. Would someone talk to her if she knocked on a door?

'They will chase you out,' her mother had warned. 'Don't you have anything else to write about?' There was a lot to write about, but this seemed to have a deep emotional connection. She had burned with the desire to write about it someday. She somehow had to see grandmother's friend Soundari Ammal, even if no one else spoke to her.

She saw the temple tower in the distance. 'That was where it all started,' her grandmother had told her. Her mother lacked her grandmother's intensity. As if she had purposely screened it from the world. This was unnecessary for mother's profession as a doctor. She had never even visited this place.

This was grandmother's birthplace. A place where, even today, there was not even a proper hotel to greet visitors. Yet, this was the place that had sparked a revolution half a century ago. A revolution spearheaded by her grandmother.

'How was this possible, grandma?' she would ask. Her grandmother would gaze into the distance. Her facial tissues would tighten. 'Some day you must go to my birthplace and see a house called Ranga Vilas in North Masi Street. The revolution was sparked in the cowshed there.'

She had gone in search of that house as soon as she had reached this place yesterday. It had been locked. She had knocked on the neighbouring house and a man had stuck his head out. 'Is there no one in the next house?'

'No,' he had responded.

'No one has lived there for several years. It belonged to a *mirasu* called Rangam Iyer. He had no children.'

'What do you mean, no children?' his wife asked, as she came to join him.

'I meant his wife had no children.'

'I would very much like to see that house,' said Mandakini. 'Who might have the key to that house?'

'Why, do you want to buy that house?'

She replied spontaneously, without thought. 'I'm writing a book about old houses in Tamil Nadu. It seems as if this house will look good inside.'

'Oh, it is a lovely house. All teakwood and marble, even at that time but there is no one to buy it. I have the keys and will show it to you.'

This was an unexpected stroke of luck. Even the door was impressive—the shining wood was intricately carved, with tiny bells hung on it. As the door was unlocked with some noise, the bells tinkled. She felt her stomach sinking as she stepped inside. As if she was intruding on the privacy of another's life. The house was clean, although it smelled slightly musty.

'I clean it every fortnight,' the man said.

The hall and walls whispered the history of a century ago. The wooden swing had brass fittings. A hazy image of the person who had used it started forming in her mind. 'That is Rangam Iyer's photo,' the man said.

She was startled at the resemblance between that face and her mother's. The same eyebrows. The same nose. The same mouth. There were many photos on the walls. Mandakini scanned them eagerly. Finally, she saw it. Her grandmother as a graduate. In the customary black dress as a graduate, holding her rolled-up certificate in her hand. Something overflowed inside her. There was also a photo of her grandmother along with her siblings. She wiped off the dust on that picture with her handkerchief.

'Who is this?' she asked.

'Rangam Iyer's children. That is, the children of the woman he "kept", devadasi,' he whispered, as if it was a forbidden word.

'Did they grow up here?'

'No way. They were not allowed to step inside the house. He was extremely orthodox, they say. He used to go to that woman's house, but it was said that he never even drank water there.'

Mandakini looked at Rangam Iyer's photo. She wondered how that 'dasi' birthed children for him.

The man opened the doors to different rooms. It was a large house. A house with sleek mosaic floors that had not felt the pattering feet of children. Walls that had not heard laughter. There were dark pillars standing like ghosts around the courtyard. The sun's rays shone like a band through the chimney, casting inexplicable shadows in the kitchen and the rear of the house.

'The cooking for dasi's house too happened here but no one would go and give the food to her. She would come and stand in the backyard to collect it.'

'I know.'

'What?'

'Strange, I said.'

'What's strange about it? That was how it was. As soon as he returned from her house, Rangam Iyer would go straight to the well, have a bath, and only then enter this house. But he did not neglect his wife. Many men those days ruined themselves and their families smitten by women of that community. This Dasi was also different. She sent all her children to a hostel and educated them using the money he gave her.'

'Let's look at the backyard.'

'What is there? Just a ruined cowshed.'

'That's alright. Let us see it.'

'As you wish.'

The big wooden door opened with a loud creak. Her heart palpitated as she stepped on the uneven stone steps and placed her foot in the backyard. A ruined, roofless cowshed with overgrown plants. A mango tree.

They were standing underneath it. The 'dasi' and her children. It was then that a tempest must have blown inside the heart of a six-year-old girl. It was then that a revolution must have been sparked in the breast of the little girl watching the humiliation.

Mandakini carefully read the name of the street, letter by letter. North Masi Street. Who would direct her to Soundari Ammal's house?

She saw a man coming towards her. He had shaded his eyes with his right hand to protect them against the blazing sun.

'Could you tell me where Soundari Ammal's house is?' she asked him.

Chellappa decided to visit Soundari Ammal that evening. Soundari Ammal had been famous four decades ago and was now almost forgotten. Why would a city girl want to see her? He should have warned that girl about Soundari Ammal's extreme pride. 'Aunt is far more courageous than any of you city girls,' he should have told her.

'No one can take advantage of this Soundari! My pride and dignity are most important to me! I stopped singing on stage for that reason.' How many had that clarity, knowledge and pride these days?

His heart skipped a beat when he saw Mallika standing in front of him. She was wiping her sweaty, red face. Soundari Ammal must have looked like Mallika at this age, he thought.

'Is a cool breeze blowing just for you?'

'No other choice. It is Saturday and college is over. I am returning home. Are you returning from the library? Couldn't you take an umbrella?'

Chellappa narrated the story of his umbrella and Mallika had a good laugh. She looked at her watch and bit her lip.

'Oh, I must go, *annachi* (brother). Senthil will get mad if I return even a little late after college. Father and aunt will not say anything but Senthil will shout at me.

'Why?'

'He seems to think he is the man of the house! Mother will dance to his tune. A real pain! They do not even allow me to learn music. There's a lot I need to talk to you...'

Chellappa was unable to find an appropriate response.

'He hates it if I even hum a song. What shall I do—I feel like singing all the time. It seems like my breath.' Mallika laughed. 'I will come by and cry to you one day. Is your wife well?'

'I think so. She has gone to her mother's house in Thiruvaroor.'

'Why don't you come to our place to eat?'

'No need. I am going to the lodge. It seems like you already have a visitor.'

'Who is that?'

'I don't know. Perhaps someone from Madras.'

'How do you know?'

'It is just a guess.'

'I see. Man or woman?'

'Female.'

'Then your guess must be right.'

Mallika gave a sudden laugh and started walking home. Chellappa thought that Senthil was as idiotic as his father Sabapathy. The thought made him angry.

His thoughts returned to his father again. A music performance had just concluded at a wedding in Thiruvaroor. Two men were debating the nuances of Dikshithar's song. Father interrupted and voiced some opinion.

'Keep quiet,' said one man.

'You are just a drummer. What do you know? Shut up,' said the other.

Father never spoke until he returned home. That night, he lay on a mat in the terrace, staring at the moon. 'Chellappa, you should not take up my profession,' he said.

'You must study. Study Sanskrit. Don't study Tamil.'

My son must become an educated man. It is my wish. No, it is a burning desire. His education is my redemption.

'Who might the visitor be?' Mallika walked at almost a run, making myriad guesses as she raced home. None of them seemed interesting. Suddenly, her legs seemed to bind together. Maybe someone had come asking for her hand? Mother was very eager to get her married. She felt irritated that Senthil was even more eager to do so. He was only four years older than her. Yet, he tried to dominate her.

'Let anyone come asking for my hand. I do not want to get married. I want to study. I want to learn music,' she muttered to herself.

It seemed definite in her imagination that someone had come asking for her hand and Senthil was guarding her on the wedding dais. She felt her temper rise. Who did Senthil think he was? He goes to movies and music performances, but I must not. I am not even allowed to sing.

'Who are you to stop me? I will sing,' she had told him one day. Mother and Senthil had become extremely agitated, as if they had seen a ghost.

'We should get her married immediately,' Senthil had said, as if a man was waiting outside the house to marry her. 'Then let her husband handle her.'

Amma had been angry too. 'Taken after her father's sister,' she had burst out.

'Please keep quiet, Karpagam,' father had chided. It was a rare occurrence. Amma had subsided after that. In her anger, Mother must have forgotten about aunt's monthly pension of a thousand rupees.

She did not know if aunt had heard all this. What she did know was that aunt was beyond all such pettiness. Aunt had been an indispensable part of the household ever since Mallika could remember. She had never heard Aunt speak about cooking, food, relationships or giving it all up. She would listen constantly to songs on the radio. She would sometimes sing to herself. Her clear, bell-like voice would make Mallika's heart overflow with joy. The photographs on the wall were proof that aunt had been a famous singer in her day. It seemed to Mallika that aunt was the queen of some kingdom, although she had never left the house for two decades and remained seated in her reclining chair.

Aunt had no husband or children. 'Her husband died,' said mother by way of explanation. However, aunt still put a big red dot on her forehead. The diamonds in her nose and ears sparkled even in the pathetic light of the 40-watt bulb in the living room.

Aunt addressed her one day, without considering that Mallika was only 12 years old.

'No one married me, my dear,' she said.

'Maybe men were afraid of your talent.'

Aunt laughed. 'I said no. I was determined to not give up my singing even if I got married. No man wanted that. No prestige in having all that knowledge if you are born in that particular community. Why, even the men of that community will bury the women they are born with.'

'Did they try to bury you?'

'They tried! But this Soundari cannot be buried so easily.'

Mallika was amused for some reason. She felt that this was a secret between aunt and her.

'Respect is different from what people believe to be. Do you understand?'

Mallika understood gradually. She got angry because Senthil did not understand and was trying to bury aunt's desires.

She stood in front of her house, even as she was thinking whether to go home or not.

'Thanks so much. Thank you,' the young woman was saying as she stepped out of the house.

'This is my daughter,' Mallika's father said. 'She is studying in Plus Two.'

'Oh, does she sing?' asked the woman.

'No, she doesn't,' said father hurriedly.

'Mallika, come in,' ordered Senthil. She went in, burning with humiliation.

'Why is Senthil making such a ruckus, aunty?'

'No idea. That girl spoke to me cordially. She even requested me to sing.'

'What do you know about journalists?' shouted Senthil. 'They'll say one thing and write something sensational.'

'She is the granddaughter of a dear friend of mine,' said Soundari pleasantly.

'That's exactly the point I'm making. We don't want *their* acquaintance.'

She vaguely understood what he was saying. But she felt weary that a young boy was talking to her in this manner.

'Hey Senthil, why don't you keep quiet? What is your age? What is aunt's age?'

Even Sabapathy's scolding seemed hypocritical and ineffective to her. Sabapathy is afraid of his son. When I die, he is completely dependent on Senthil.

A soft hand touched her forearm. She turned around.

'You said she was your friend's granddaughter. Who is this friend?' whispered Mallika. Soundari smiled a little.

'I'll tell you another day, dear.'

The landing was getting dark. Someone switched on the light. Soundari could not believe that she had just met Rathnam's granddaughter.

It seemed as if 50 years and more had dissolved as that girl spoke. She could still see Rathnam's dignity, anger, indignation and courage.

❧

'A huge scam is going on in God's name, Soundari.' When the words burst out of Rathnam, Soundari's finger, which was tuning the tambura, stilled.

'No other country treats its women this way in the name of tradition and culture. Wake up. This society is taking advantage of us, giving us diseases, and humiliating us.' Her face would redden. The glasses she wore—no other girl in the town wore them—would slip down her nose.

'You are an educated woman, Rathnam. Still, how many people will listen to you?'

'It won't happen if I speak alone of course. We should all raise our voices. We should stand at the crossroads and fight for our rights.'

Soundari had felt like laughing then. 'At the crossroads?'

'Yes. They threw our dignity into the crossroads. Do we have any respect in this society? You are such a famous singer. Dhanam is a fantastic dancer. They call you for music performances and weddings. Did you notice where they feed you? Somewhere in the backyard—never in the dining room with the others.'

Soundari could not respond to her. If Soundari said, 'Hasn't it always been like this?', 'Who gave them the right,' she would retort. 'God? Did God ask us to dance in the temple before every ritual?' she would ask. 'Did God tell us to get married to a stone idol after which any man can take you to bed?' she would fume. Call yourself devadasi—servants of God, ha, it is not god that you serve but ...'

Her rants could not be stopped.

'Many women have been victimized because of this. They have suffered and destroyed others as well. This should not continue, Soundari.'

There was some magic in her words. So many women came, as if bound by a spell. Like they were getting ready for a freedom fight.

That was when Dhanam stopped dancing. I could support them in every way but could not stop singing. 'You have to make sacrifices during a struggle, Soundari.' I could not. My sorrow overwhelmed me when I thought about it. Rathnam left when I told her I would rather drink poison and die.

'Get married and continue singing,' she said. As if someone was ready to marry me.

'Aunt, why did you stop singing on stage?' asked Mallika.

Soundari felt weary suddenly. There was a desperation burning in her stomach after all these years. Some scoundrel is asking her to sing *Manmatha Leelai*, an obscene song from a movie. He is saying something vulgar. The crowd is laughing. She could not understand if she felt sorrow or anger.

She had stopped performing then. Rathnam had been right after all.

'I just stopped I guess.'

'You'll talk about it in a magazine interview, but you won't tell me.'

'Who is interviewing?' asked Chellappa, as he came in.

Soundari welcomed him. 'Malika is asking why I stopped singing.'

'You don't know how much self-respect your aunt has,' said Chellappa.

'What's the use of my self-respect? Talk about Rathnam's,' said Soundari.

'How come you remembered Rathnam today?'

'Her granddaughter was here this afternoon to interview me.'

Chellappa opened his eyes wide.

'Oh, was that Rathnam's granddaughter? What did she ask?'

'She asked me about what it was like then. Why should I hesitate to talk to my friend's granddaughter? That is why Senthil is raging like an earthquake.'

After some time, Chellappa left, deep in thought. At the crossroads, he could still hear the shouts of the crowd Rathnam had gathered. He was amazed when his father, too, had joined the crowd and raised his voice in support. Those voices drowned the sound of dancing bells and the tambura and the music with it. The entire street emptied out. They triumphed over their mental demons, lived normal lives, and had families. The community had been granted dignity, at last. No longer dasis—not even to God. To utter the word was blasphemous. They did not need to raise their voices anymore. This place would not witness anymore shattering earthquakes.

But the earth did shatter a fortnight later. Senthil entered the house like a hurricane and flung a magazine on the ground.

'Gone. Our dignity and prestige are gone. Look!' he raged, addressing his aunt. 'We can't face the world anymore. Mallika will never get married...'

Everyone looked terrified. Senthil then did what he had never done before. He sat down on a stool and covered his face. Then he cried, his body racked with sobs. Those sobs were even more terrifying than his anger.

Soundari felt a chill down her spine. What now? 'What, what is written in that magazine?'

'They have tom-tommed all about your community, our ancestry to the world. Didn't I tell you not to give an interview?'

The magazine still lay on the ground, like it was on fire. No one dared touch it.

'Mallika, please read it,' said Soundari weakly.

Mallika was shocked at Senthil's tantrums and tears.

'Is there anything about our community?'

'Yes, there is, in the very heading.'

'Isn't there anything else?'

Senthil hissed furiously. 'So, what if there is? What if they have praised your music? Is that of any consequence?'

Soundari sat still, stunned. Sabapathy was quiet, head bowed. Karpagam stood panting, as if unable to demonstrate her anger but satisfied with Senthil's outburst.

'What can I do, Senthil?' asked Soundari quietly. 'Bring me poison if you want. I will drink it and die.'

Only Mallika felt like crying when she heard this.

There was no need for anyone to bring poison. Soundari Ammal died in her sleep the following night. At least, that is what the doctor said. When Sabapathy went to clean out his sister's shelf of belongings 10 days later, he saw a prescription for sleeping pills. The question was how they came into Soundari's possession, because she was never in the habit of taking sleeping pills.

Sabapathy never opened his mouth. Mallika's wedding did not happen in the auspicious month of *thai* that year. When Chellappa asked her if she needed his help to join a music class, Mallika's reply was categorical: 'No, thanks. I don't want to even think about it.'

Original Tamil title: *Chinnam*
Translated by: Sukanya Venkataraman
First published in *Guftugu*, June 2021, https://guftugu.in/2021/06/11/the-symbol/

# Dance of the Gods

They were dancing at a distance—going round in big immaculate circles, beating the drum tied to each of their waists. Keeping to the beat, swaying their bodies forward and backward; still moving, each of them lifted his long red sash and gracefully rotated it over his head—the sheer beauty of the movement took her breath away. Brown naked chests and shoulders glistening with sweat; but the faces were grim without a smile. Wasn't it a joy to dance? Madhappan should be there. Won't *he* at least smile? No face was clearly visible. No, not when the dance was so far away.

There was no way she could go near to watch. That is how it had to be. She was not to be seen by the dancers either. When she came here as a new bride, she thought it was queer. She no longer asks the stupid question 'Why can't I go near and watch the dance?' She has learnt to remain mute like the other women here.

The beat of the drums—there was no music or song; just the sound of the drums—how did it create such a mesmerising rhythm? Her body swayed and her feet started patting the mud underneath. *Thai, thai,* and *thaam*—right, left and pause. At ease. Again. Right, left...

'Hey, Panchali, what is wrong with you?'

She turned. Athai Rakkammaa, the elder aunt, always ill-tempered, admonishing.

Panchali smiled. 'Nothing! Oh, my feet? Don't you feel like tapping them sometimes?'

The women who stood near her covered their mouths with their saris to hide their smiles.

'No!' said Rakkammaa fiercely. 'If you can't stand still, go inside!'

Panchali felt like answering back. Sita, who stood next to her, pinched her waist, reminding her to keep quiet. She bent her head in shame and was irritated. They were dancing at a distance. It no longer interested her. She felt there was no connection between them and her. In the stories her mother would tell her, there would be ghosts and fairies. She understood that they were different from human beings. She did not know who they, dancing there, were. Somebody. They called it 'dance of the gods'. Gods—were they? She slipped away silently and walked towards her single-room house.

The area was a huge dense jungle full of trees, cool and shady. It appeared seamless. She has many times desired to walk the length and breath of it or fly, spreading her arms wide, like a bird. But she would be able to do that only if she turned into a spirit, a ghost. She has heard there were sentinels guarding all corners of the place. 'They had eagle eyes,' warned Sita, whom she addressed as *akka* (elder sister).

The ground below was cool. There was a cold breeze that made her shiver inside her thin sari that covered her naked breasts. She, like the other women here did not wear a blouse. She wondered if those teak-coloured bare-chests did not feel the cold. Will I ever be able to watch their dance from near? Oh, she will have to turn into a spirit for that too. What kind of a place is this? She kicked a piece of stone at her feet that flew up and fell somewhere. Her sari covering her breast slipped. She felt someone was looking at her. She hurriedly covered her breasts and looked up. A man was standing across the fence. She could not see his face clearly in the mist-covered darkness of the woods.

'Who are you angry with?'

She was absolutely shocked. She did not know if it was anger or panic that made her pick up a piece of stone and throw it at him. He laughed and moved away. She felt she had heard that voice before. She was terrified and began to run as fast as she could navigate through the woods, her heart pounding.

There never was a fence in *her* village. Though her people too were ignorant of the outside world, they didn't barricade themselves with fences all round. As it was here—seven-foot-high, tightly secured, barbed wire fences. She noticed that even on the very first day when she stepped in here with the wedding garland of tuberoses still fresh round her neck.

She had asked her neighbour, Sita akka, 'What is this heavy fencing for? Are there wild animals around? I feel I have entered a cage!'

Sita smiled. 'That is exactly what it is. We cannot step outside. Nor can any outsider get in.'

'Why?'

'That is the tradition here. It has been so always, they say, laid out by our ancestors.'

'What about men? Are they also not allowed to go?'

'They do. But there are restrictions for them too,' Sita akka had lowered her voice to a whisper.

'No outsider can come?'

'No, not even the police!'

She laughed. 'Is it such a peaceful place then?'

'Nothing will go beyond this fence,' whispered Sita. 'Whatever happens, there is an elder's court—a panchayat—that solves the problems.'

There were many cages. There was one for women during their menstrual periods. The kitchen was another. But that was funny. No male, not even the husband could enter the kitchen. 'Do they fear that they would be given some work to do?' she had laughed. It was only in the night that there was any contact with the man. In the pitch darkness of the still night. Many nights she could not even be sure if it was the man she was wedded to.

Did *Amma*, her mother, know about the customs here when she hurriedly married her off? Why was she in such a tearing hurry? Now it seemed to her that the rogue she was reminded of today might have been the reason. Amma did not ask her nor did she ask her mother why she decided and fixed the marriage. She had actually no role to play. That is how it was. 'You shall marry,' they said and so she did. Amma never came here after the wedding. Her daughter now belonged to another house. There were so many questions that needed to be asked. Did Amma really not know the traditions of this place? Amma must have known and yet… how did she…? How many enemies does she have? Amma now stood as the prime accused. When she heard that fellow's laughter today, it was Amma who came to her mind. If her mother had stood before her, she would have twisted her neck like Sita's husband breaks the neck of a hen. Amma who told her stories—there was a story for every blessed thing. Story of Rama, Sita, Panchali...

'How do you know so many stories Amma? Who told you these stories?'

'My grandfather. He would recite stories in the village, after the lamps were lit, as darkness covered the streets. People would gather round him to listen. Storytelling would go on sometimes till dawn. I grew up listening to stories.'

Every time the story would change and take new forms, according to Amma's mood. Amma loved the story of Panchali. 'No one should suffer the plight that she faced,' she would say.

'Then why did you name me after her?'

'I didn't; it was the choice of my mother-in-law'

'It was not a name, but a curse,' she thinks. 'Why didn't you visit me? Did they forbid you too?'

Something stuck to her foot. She bent to see what it was. It was a plump, ripe, dark-skinned jamun fruit, fallen from the tree. Its juice had spread a dark patch at the bottom of her foot. She looked up and was surprised to see the tree that had escaped her attention before. There was quite a lot of jamun fruit on the ground glistening in the grass. She picked a few and hid them in the folds of her pallu. She put a couple in her mouth and sucked the juice. She remembered Amma had a story for the jamun tree too. It was again another of Panchali's.

'Panchali went for a stroll one day. She sees a shining fruit hanging. Unable to control the desire to eat it, she plucks it and is about to eat when Krishna comes and says, 'Oh, it belongs to a hermit and is forbidden for anyone to pluck it. If he knows that you have plucked it, he will curse not only you but also your husbands.' Panchali panics. 'What do I do now?' she asks. 'You must not have any secret in your heart. If there is, you must spell it out to your husbands. Then the fruit by itself will return to the tree,' says Krishna. Panchali goes and reveals her secret to her husbands, then the fruit goes back to the tree.'

She laughed. 'What a stupid story, can anyone believe this?'

'It happened those days, dear girl.'

'You and your story—as if you were a witness to it. Well, what was the secret?'

Amma laughed. 'Panchali told her husbands, "I do not love any of you. I love Karna, your foe!"'

She laughed. 'But didn't she tell Karna that she would not marry him because he was not born a prince?'

'But she must have felt later that only he was a true male.'

'The others?'

'Impotent cowards!'

'All the five?

'Of course. Haven't I told you the story? Have you forgotten? The eldest of them loses her in a gamble. She is dragged to the court by the enemy and stripped in front of the courtiers. All of them, all the five husbands, sat with their heads bent—useless duffers!' There was real anger in Amma's voice. When she narrated the story it sounded so true.

'Why did she marry all the five in the first place?'

'Ah, ask me why. It was the folly of their mother.'

It was the folly of mothers that was responsible for the grief of all the Panchalis, she now feels.

She looked up at the tree. Streams of light came through the branches making her squint. She felt her mother was peeping from above. She felt like screaming, 'Why didn't you come to see me?' She sat on the ground and buried her face in her folded legs and closed her eyes. In its darkness she could see faces, demons that terrified her.

'Panchali was brave in the midst of her troubles,' Amma said. 'How? How could she, when she was wedded to five men? Brave? Should it not have been hate? Anger? Didn't she feel like running away? Why didn't she say, "You cowards, I will go to Karna?'" This is one of the many lies that Amma has told her. Panchali was a coward. A fool. Amma had also narrated the end of the story. "Leave her behind, she never had love for us," said all the husbands and departed for heaven or hell following a dog. Panchali was left behind like an orphaned corpse.'"

'Panchali deserved it,' she muttered as she lifted her head. Amma seemed to be looking down from the tree. Tears welled in her eyes. 'You will not come, I know. You have no courage to see me. You will surely go to hell.' As she cried silently the world had become still. The sound of a thud woke her with a start. A jamun fruit had fallen next to her. She must have fallen asleep on the cool grass. The beat of the drums had stopped. The dance must have ended. She had to reach home before the menfolk returned. She stood up took off her pallu and dusted off the grass and fruit that were stuck to the sari and covered her breasts again, tucking it securely at her waist.

'I must make millet gruel today,' she murmured to herself. Darkness had fallen quite a long time ago. She waited hungry and sleepy for Madhappan and as she was about to fall asleep, he entered silently.

He did not reply to her 'Why so late?' and started eating. She did not ask him again. She was tired and wanted to go to bed. Finishing her meal, she snuggled next to him. His warmth was comforting in the cold. 'This is real,' she felt. She wanted to tell him about the man who was near the fence and say, 'You have to tackle the rogue before he comes again.'

Madhappan was lost in thought and she decided to tell him later. She closed her eyes and held him tight. He said in a matter of fact tone, 'I am going to the city tomorrow.'

She sat up startled. With eyes wide open she asked, 'When will you be back?'

'I don't know. Maybe after two to three days.'

She struck her head fiercely with both her palms. 'Take me with you. I can't stay here.'

'Don't be a fool Panchali, you know that is not possible.'

Her body froze in fear. 'No I can't. You do not understand.' She started sobbing.

'Now look, you have to abide by the custom here. You are not a unique person. Don't cry and create a scene—you are obnoxious'.

'It is your custom that is obnoxious!' she said, raising her voice.

He slapped her hard on the face. 'If you open your mouth I will kill you.'

She covered her burning cheek with her palm and heaving with anger looked at his back as he lay in bed facing the wall. How could he sleep? She wanted to bash his back and ask him if he thought everything was fine. She was surprised that he, supposedly better educated than the others was inert to the goings on, like a donkey that carried a load, not questioning.

'You are a coward,' she said under her breath. She could coin a number of obscene curses that came to her tongue. She wondered how she would manage once he left for the city. She was haunted by strange dreams all through the night, demons chasing her from one end of the fence to another. When she opened her eyes the next morning Madhappan had left.

After having her morning gruel, she went to gather dry twigs for the oven, with the single question tormenting her brain. 'What am I going to do?' As she broke the twigs, a twig pierced her thigh and she saw a drop of blood oozing from it. She gazed at it for some time and pierced the little cut deeper. There was more blood now and she quickly smeared it on the sari that covered her buttocks. It was a light blue sari by chance. The bloodstain was visible. She heard someone laugh. She turned her head frightened. There was no one. She hurried home, kept the bundle of twigs in the corner of the kitchen, closed the door and walked slowly to the hut meant for seclusion during the menstrual period. She was relieved to see Sita sitting there. She could even smile a little. Sita was surprised to see her.

'Why Panchali, didn't you just have your periods a fortnight ago?'

'I don't know akka, it has come early this time. My whole body aches.'

'Then just lie down. Here is the mat. The floor is cold.'

Panchali lay on the mat gratefully and asked, 'All of you seem to remember when women here have their periods, as if you have no other thought.'

Sita laughed. 'There is nothing else really. You sleep. I will inform that we need food for you.'

She was relieved that she was able to manage her problem for now. She fell asleep due to the lack of sleep the previous night. When she woke up, there was food kept in front of her. Sita sat looking intently at her.

'Have you eaten Akka? 'she asked feeling embarrassed.

'No, we will eat together, go wash your face.'

Sita waited for her to finish her meal and asked gently. 'Has Madhappan gone out of the village?'

'Yes akka, how do you know?'

'These things are not hard to find out. Rakkammaa aunt told me. She asked, 'How come Panchali has her period so early?'

She did not answer. She went to wash her hands, washed the vessels, brought them back and placed them to dry and sat hugging her folded knees.

'For how long will Madhappan be away?'

'Two to three days, he said.'

'Next time when he goes, what are you going to do?'

She did not know what to say. She buried her head in her knees. 'What will I do, what will I do?' Tears rolled down her cheeks.

'All of us have tried this but we cannot escape, Panchali.'

Her chest heaved and she gasped for breath. 'Why akka, why? Is it fair?'

Sita did not answer. She probably feared that the walls had ears.

Sita akka's seclusion would be over tomorrow and she would be left alone. Sita was the only person who was empathetic.

'How old is your marriage akka?'

'Four years.'

'God, and you grew up here!'

'I am wise, therefore. I have understood that nothing belongs to us.'

Panchali shook her head. 'I was not aware of that. I am Panchali just in name.'

Sita smiled with a vacant stare. 'Rakkamma aunt says that we are descendants of Panchali. It is the tribe's custom that we follow. Defying that, we shall be cursed.'

Panchali tried to say something, when Sita pressed her palm across her mouth. 'Look, you should not speak on this hereafter. Don't you drag me into your problem.'

As darkness fell and they lay silently on their mats, demons watched from the nooks and corners of the hut. Strong cold winds banged at the door as if they were carriers of an ominous message—You own nothing, nothing at all…

When Panchali woke up the next morning Sita had gone. The next day and the day after two women joined her in seclusion. They remained silent all day. It looked like they had never spoken in their lives. Weren't they ever embarrassed? They were from here born and bred. It would never occur to them to question. She was the odd one out. An outsider, an embarrassment.

On the fourth day Panchali had her bath and entered her house, relieved at the thought that Madhappan would return that night.

Rakkamma aunt confronted Panchali on the way. Nodding her head she said, 'Madhappan is coming back today,' in a threatening tone.

It sent a chill down Panchali's spine. 'What is she trying to say?' She wondered what the old woman was up to. She walked fast. 'Everything would be fine in a few hours,' she said to herself.

As evening dissolved into twilight she finished cooking and got ready to freshen up. For Madhappan, her husband, still a stranger. She washed her face with a scented soap. She wore the soft nylex sari that Madhappan liked. She lit the earthen lamp and waited. Hours dragged on but there was no sign of Madhappan. Fear gripped her. 'Will he not come today? But he will, didn't Rakkamma say so?' She felt hungry and ate a little to appease it and lay on the mat. 'Let him come whenever,' she muttered and fell asleep.

Amma came in and sat before her. Panchali was gripped with anger. 'Did you come to tell me your stories? Go away. I don't need them, sorry.'

There was a sad smile on Amma's lips. 'Not a story dear, the truth.'

'What is the truth?"

'Truth till today.'

'Didn't you say it was the mother's fault?'

'Yes, but, would she have said, "Whatever it is, share it among yourselves equally," if she had known what it was to be shared?'

'Amma, go away before I break your neck. Your Panchali had five, I have four. That is the only difference. When Madhappan goes out to town, every night there is one waiting to enter. Go away. Don't give me an excuse that you didn't know. Go, go away.' Her voice broke into myriads of hoarse sounds like an animal, wounded.

There was a repeated knock on the door. She sat up with a start. The knocking stopped abruptly. Someone entered like a shadow. She found a figure sitting in the faint light shed by the earthen lamp. She was terrified. Who is it? Slowly the mist in her eyes cleared. It was Madhappan.

She heaved a sigh of relief. She smiled. 'When did you come? Why are you sitting like this?' she asked cheerfully.

His face looked tense. What now? 'What happened during my absence?'

'I had my periods. I had my bath only this morning.'

'Is it true?'

'Why do you ask?' she asked cautiously.

'I hear a lot of things about you.'

'Like what?'

'Whatever. Discipline is important here.'

'What does it mean?'

'You should not lie. You have to listen to the elders.'

She did not answer. She was almost choked by anger that was building up inside. She bent her head not wanting to even look at his face.

'Who is he?'

She looked up caught unawares. 'Who?'

'I hear that he stands near the fence. And you stand showing him your breasts.'

A sudden rage inflamed the pit of her stomach. 'You fool, you will be cursed!' she fumed. 'Who told you?'

'Shut up bitch!' he screamed. 'Picking up twigs is not what you do over there, I know. Raising your sari above your thighs, rolling on the grass under the jamun tree...what is it? Are you a whore?'

The fire at the pit of the stomach rose to her heart, throat and head.

'Who is he, tell me!' he roared, slapping her. 'The elders are convening the Panchayat tomorrow. My honour is at stake. I cannot save you.'

She suddenly wanted to laugh. Spit fire. She rose from the floor. 'I will tell you, yes I will. It is the secret that Panchali had in her heart. It is the same. That fellow is here. I will bring him to you. Just sit here.'

Her whole body seemed to be on fire. She ran out of the house and entered the kitchen where no male could enter and locked the door. The twigs that she had piled waited for her. With the drop of a matchstick it caught fire embracing her in its fumes.

They stood mute and watched—Madhappan and his brothers—the tongues of flames that leapt through the thatched roof towards the sky, with a fury that was audible in the silence of the dead night.

She walked at ease, spreading her arms like the wings of a bird measuring the length and breath of the forest. At the break of dawn, there began the sound of the drums. They were dancing—going round in big immaculate circles beating the drum tied to their waist. Keeping to the beat, swaying their bodies forward and backward; still moving, each of them lifted his long red sash and gracefully rotated it over his head—the sheer beauty of the movement took her breath away. Brown naked chests and shoulders glistening with sweat. She could see them now clearly.

Original Tamil title: *Avalathu Antharangam*
Translated by the author.

# Gap

The dream engulfed him until he was prodded awake with a stick. He was still smiling from the memory of his dream. He was sitting like a dot, a point in the center of a long row of flower shops. She was standing beyond mountains of flowers, like a flower herself. Like her name. Gulabi. Rose.

Garlands of yellow marigolds and red roses hung in chains, swinging when people jostled them. He gazed at her silken face amidst them, unashamed. Her beetle-dark eyes eagerly scanned the mountains of flowers. Her pomegranate lips smiled in awe. Was there ever such a wonder in Allah's creations? How would it be if he touched her? He extended his hand.

'Hey, wake up. Are you dreaming?'

The cane prodded his waist painfully. He woke up with a start. He saw the cane first. Like an unravelling film reel, the dim light revealed Javdekar in his police uniform with his sharp eyes and a mocking smile beneath his moustache. He sat up on his side, fearfully. What was Javdekar here for today? Would his antics start early in the day?

'Didn't I tell you to get up?

The others in the room were still asleep.

He held onto his long shorts, which were slipping, and tied them. The tie-up cord was frayed at the ends. Before he could stand upright, he felt a sting on his knee. The same place that he had been struck yesterday.

'Come on. Got the news last night that you are being freed today.'

He looked around, bewildered. Was this being told to him or was it meant for someone else? The others were curled up, eyes closed.

'What are you gaping for? Are you happy hearing this or not? You must give me something for telling you this good news. Ok, now move...'

He walked as if in a dream. When would the news have been transmitted? Before he was hit or after? He felt like taking a pee.

'I'll take a pee and be back,' he said, his head bent as if he was mortified to say so.

'Ok, go and then come to the office room.'

He could not see the path to the restroom in the dawning light but walked swiftly towards it on instinct. Initially the smell would turn his stomach. Now nothing bothered his senses. He opened the tap in the lavatory and washed his face. The cold water felt good. It seemed to penetrate his brain and move aside the cobwebs there ever so slightly. The sky was turning grey when he walked out and looked up.

What did Javdekar say?

'You are being freed today.'

Was it the truth? Or was it another trick to beat him up further?

He hesitantly went and lingered by the office room door. The warden was sitting at his table. His face seemed less harsh today.

'Come, Ayub Khan. Come in and sign your name. You can go home today.'

'Why now, out of the blue?' he wanted to ask, but did not. He signed where they asked him to. He saw the picture of an adolescent boy on the form. It seemed like someone else. He bent down and peered at it. Javdekar and the warden looked at each other, smiled and shook their heads.

'Here is the money you earned here.'

He accepted the money and counted it. Two thousand and eight rupees. It seemed like a lot of money. All new notes. He was afraid to even touch it.

Javdekar held out a small package. 'Your clothes. See if they still fit you.'

He went aside and tried to wear his clothes. The shirt was tight. His waist was too big for his shorts. He pulled the rope from his long shorts and wound it around his waist. Javdekar laughed.

'Go get yourself a lungi. Or you'll find one at home. Your house is here, right?'

He shook his head to indicate no.

'Then where is it?'

He did not respond. That was his private business. Instead, he shrugged. The warden looked at his file. 'Mysore,' he said with some surprise.

'Great! Then buy a lungi here,' said Javdekar. 'Many buses go to Bangalore. Take a bus from there and go home.'

'Who is there at home?'

He turned around, stunned. Yes, it was the warden who had asked him. He had never experienced anything but harshness in that man.

He thought for a bit. It seemed like the cobwebs were suffocating his brain again. He closed his eyes in thought. He saw a big inner courtyard. He saw every face, dull like an old family photo. The courtyard was bright. As if the sun was resting there…

'Well, go on then. Don't get into any trouble from now on.'

He started again, wondering how to respond. He moved to leave the room in silence, still doubting his freedom.

'Ayub! Do you know why they freed you?' asked the warden.

He shook his head to indicate no.

'The court decided that you were not guilty.'

Ayub looked at the warden in surprise.

'Today is August 15th. Independence Day. You are also free and independent. Aren't you happy?'

He did not know. It seemed like they were mocking him. He felt unreasonably agitated. His heart palpitated. His blood rushed to the nape of his neck and his face grew warm. How does happiness feel?

'Go on now. Go home. Make an honest living and survive.'

He came out. He had seen similar scenes in many Hindi movies. A girlfriend or friend would be waiting to welcome the prisoner. The entrance was devoid of life and there was no one.

His shorts hurt his waist since they were too tight. He would have to wait until the shops opened. Footpath shops could be cheaper.

Mumbai was not yet awake. He was surprised to see so little traffic. The Mumbai he remembered had been bustling, crowded and dirty. The opposite of Mysore. The streets of Mysore were wide with cooling trees on either side. The streets were clean. It was a quiet town with gentle folk. But he had liked Mumbai. He had been awestruck by its speed. It seemed like yesterday when he had stared with an open mouth at everything, like a villager who comes to a city for the first time. Gaping at the sea. At the massive cinema posters. At the urchins standing outside the sky-high walls of movie star bungalows waiting for a glimpse of them. At multi-storey buildings and the wealthy residing in them. Streets with buried secrets. The *pav bhaji*[1] in street side shops…the filth piled in corners. Dogs and cows hovering around plastic bottles and bags…the casual indifference of people who always seemed to be in a hurry…the celebratory laugh of the frothing ocean…

Nothing registered today. A sleepy Mumbai seemed strange. Like a dull piece of art, its paint faded and peeling.

1 *Pav bhaji*: a street food dish consisting of a bun served with vegetable curry.

He walked where his feet led him. The sea breeze wafted in. He saw smoke in a corner tea shop. There were two others when he reached it. He got a paper cup of tea, along with some change, for ten rupees. Masala tea. The fragrance wafted into his very being. He savoured its heat with closed eyes as it penetrated his body. The shopkeeper laughed when Ayub opened his eyes.

'Do you need another chai?' he asked in Marathi.

He thought about it but decided to have one at breakfast instead and continued walking. The ocean seemed to come closer as he walked on. Mumbai started to bustle again as more pedestrians and vehicles began plying the streets. He noticed that the seaside street shops were open and walked towards them. Jeans and tee shirts were in huge piles.

'Get yourself a lungi,' Javdekar had said. He was not used to wearing a lungi. The boy at the street shop selected a pair of jeans and a tee that would fit him. The boy sold them for 80 rupees after intense bargaining. 'Ok, you are my first sale of the day,' he reasoned. Ayub felt new energy inside him after changing into his new outfit in a fairly private space.

He discarded his old clothes in a street corner trash pile and moved forward. He sat on the parapet wall near the sea and gazed at it. The horizon glittered like diamonds, as if the sun was sitting on the waves. Those closer to the shore seemed a darker blue. He stared at them vacantly for a while.

He felt stunned. It seemed as if he and the universe were standing still. Gulabi came floating on the waves. 'Do you remember me, Gulab?' She laughed her tinkling laugh. 'How can I remember you when I never knew you?'

He felt cheated and buried his head in his knees. His memories lengthened, like a long list. They expanded with those he had seen in the sun-lit inner courtyard. They would remember him for sure. Vappa, Amma-*jaan*, Bhai-*jaan*...would they remember him? The courtyard spun below his head. The aroma of Amma-*jaan*'s kothu parotta beckoned him.

'Come Ayub, I have made *kurma*[2] just the way you like it. With coconut milk...'

Tears flooded his eyes and spilled over. Will you recognize me now? Will you make parotta with kurma for me?

He wondered where all these tears had been before today. He allowed it to flow and ebb on its own. Sunlight stung his neck. He stroked it, looking up. He wiped his face and eyes.

A boy was sitting in the vicinity. He laughed at Ayub. 'Why are you crying? If you need a job, I can get one for you.'

Ayub got up hurriedly and walked on without replying.

'Hey, are you deaf or dumb?'

That boy reminded Ayub of himself. He turned around and looked at the boy who was wearing Ayub's discarded shirt and shorts. He felt like giving a resounding slap on the boy's back.

In truth, it seemed like he had forgotten how to use words. He felt like he could not utter even a single sentence. It had been days since he had spoken...He had forgotten if it

2 *Kurma*: curry made of meat or vegetables cooked with yogurt.

had been days or years. He vowed to never open his mouth until he left Mumbai.

He joined the long queue at the bus stop. He understood that the arriving bus was going to Dadar railway station. He boarded it. It felt like an invisible hand was shoving him.

His body and brain worked like a machine. The crowd inside the railway station left him breathless. Waves of unstopping humanity flowed forward like a deluge. He reached the ticket counter, floating on that wave. The man at the counter must be a robot. He took the money and issued tickets in silence. His speed, heavy silence, and his betel-leaf chewing mouth agitated Ayub. After asking several times and getting scolded, he got a ticket to Mysore.

Sweat poured down his forehead as if he had run a mile. The train departed only in the evening. He came out and started eating the pav bhaji at the corner shop with relish. His stomach shamelessly asked for more, regardless of how much he ate. Mango juice –*Aam ras*. His mind was saturated with happiness.

'Are you happy now?'

It seemed like this was happiness. It seemed like a new invention. He could not believe it. No fear of Javdekar's cane or the mockery of others…No need to try and hide from their unbridled atrocities…How had this become possible?

'The court has decided that you are not guilty.'

You bastards…Climbing up and down endless steps of wandering, onlookers spitting on him and lowering his head because he was unable to digest it…the countless ups and downs of that rutted, rough path were branded in his brain… That walk had aged him inside and out…It was a scene out of a movie. An absurd, unbelievable story. He was the loser hero of that story.

He wanted to laugh out loud till he shook. It could have been that he wanted to cry too. He got up when he saw some young men at the next table staring at him. They would laugh if he told them his story. They would not believe him. 'Do you think we are fools?' they would ask.

This was his private humiliation. There was no need to tell anyone. Everyone would ask when he went home. What should he say? The truth?

'Is that you Ayub? Where did you disappear to? Everyone thought you were dead…'

This was more or less like death. 'Are you Ayub's ghost?' they would laugh. 'Yes, I am a ghost,' he told himself. The old Ayub is dead. He had carried him and thrown himself away. Like discarding that old shirt and shorts. Now there is a different person inside. He was worried if they would accept him. Amma-*jaan* came to mind. His stomach churned and his eyes filled. She would need to believe him. She would believe him even if no one else did, he consoled himself.

He rose and searched for a tap to wash his hands. There was a tiny wash basin in an isolated area with a mirror hanging above it. The face in that mirror was that of a stranger. He washed his face thoroughly and arranged his hair using his wet hand. He felt stronger after wiping his face with the handkerchief he had bought in a street shop. He did not know how to spend his time until evening. There was a park a short distance away. He sat on a bench there. He could see a school opposite it. The national flag was visible above its walls. He could hear students singing the national anthem. What was it today? Oh, August 15th. The warden would hoist a flag too.

He buried his head in his knees. '*Jhanda ooncha rahe hamara...*'[3] He was running carrying the flag, like in A.R. Rehman's '*Maa tujhe salaam*' music video. His heart rose higher and higher.

'*Maa tujhe salaam...*' He was wearing a Gandhi cap. His friend Basavappa was running with him. Basavappa would always wear *vibhuthi* (holy ash) on his forehead. His family would buy flowers for divine offerings from Vappa's shop. Their fathers were dear friends. And so were he and Basavappa, always together, used to sit next to each other in school.

Would Basavappa recognize him now? Would he hug Ayub like in the old days? An entire eon had slipped by since then. Beliefs and relationships would have disappeared along the way too. He felt like crying again for no reason. As if weeping for someone who was dead.

He composed himself and rose. Children in uniform were emerging from the school laughing and chittering. He looked at them eagerly for a while and then started walking back towards the railway station. He remembered how he had been unable to leave for Mysore earlier. Now,

---

3 *Jhanda ooncha rahe hamara*: May our flag always fly high.

he would have to ensure he left before anything similar happened again.

The railway coach bound for Mysore was empty. He had got a nice window seat with a sleeper. He bought a meal packet for dinner, returned to his seat, and leaned against it. It seemed strange that he had been unaware of this fact—of sitting on a train to Mysore—until early this morning.

The coach started filling up. These people lived defined lives. They knew what they would do tomorrow. He was impatient for the train to leave. Every delay meant his departure was doubtful. A khaki uniform might ask him to leave, press the nape of his neck and order 'Walk to the station.' Thank God, the train moved. Finally. He looked at the receding outer world for a while. Mysore was at the end of this journey.

He ate and lay down. Sleep made his eyes heavy, but he was afraid to sleep. Ghosts would surround him as soon as he closed his eyes. They would threaten him, whip in hand. 'Who are you, Ayub Khan? Tell us! Which gang do you belong to? Who are you?'

Blood would pour out of his cracked back. He would forget who he was in his hazy consciousness as they repeated that question. He would even forget his name. He once said his name was Basavappa. 'Are you lying, you rascal!' Oh God! The beatings made him feel like his hands, legs, and back had been ripped apart.

Hometown streets came chasing the ghosts today. Vappa and Amma came running towards him. Devaraj market expanded without end. Vappa was sitting amidst a pile of flowers and hollering in Kannada. 'Quarter kg *malligae*[4] is 20 rupees! Quarter kg rose is 10 rupees! Come! Come!' His elder brother Ahmed was dragging him along. 'Come on, we need to string many garlands. Tomorrow is Lord Ganesha's festival.' Buyers were grabbing garlands even as he strung them. He waited. Gulabi came. She was not smiling. She shrugged.

'Al Qaeda or Indian Mujahudeen? Who are you? Tell us!'

*Saare jahan se achaa...Hindustan hamara. Janda ooncha rahe hamara...*He was holding a flag like in A.R. Rehman's song.

It was bright when he opened his eyes. He sat up with a start. 'Did we pass Bangalore?' he asked the old man sitting opposite him.

'Sure, half an hour ago. Do you need to go there?'

'No, Mysore.'

'How come you slept like a person who has never slept for years?'

He went to the lavatory without responding. His very blood cells seemed jolted awake as they neared Mysore. His mind was restless. The climate had changed considerably. There was a strong, cool breeze. His palms sweated despite that.

He looked around with yearning when the train arrived in Mysore. It seemed as if there was no connection between the bursting Mumbai station and this calmer one. He was

4 *Mallige*: jasmine flowers.

overcome with emotion and his eyes filled when he stepped onto the ground. Which demon had lured him there?

He emerged from the station and took a deep breath. The palace was a short distance away. Beautiful, like a pearl. Krishna Devaraja Wadiyar's statue was at the crossroads. Devaraj Ars Road was in the vicinity. Devaraj market was beyond that. The place where his Vappa and Ahmad sold flowers. They would be there now. He wanted to see them. He would understand the situation more if he went home first.

Ayub felt an unusual thrill and sense of safety among the bustling market crowds. He realized his manic hunger and that he was standing in front of a hotel only when the smell of puri and masala wafted towards him. He was unaware if breakfast would be ready at home at this time. He entered the hotel, which seemed new, and ordered a cup of coffee along with dosa. He looked around sharply but did not see any familiar face. Or maybe no one recognized him.

He closed his eyes and leaned against the chair. He was back in town. His birthplace. Among familiar, simple people. He was the son of respected flower seller Mehboob Khan. The prodigal had returned. Like a lamb returning to its fold.

Someone touched his shoulder. His shoulders tensed in involuntary fear. He opened his eyes, startled.

'Ayub?'

A man with holy ash on his forehead was standing in front of him. Recognition hit.

'Basavappa?'

Ayub got up swiftly, stretching forward to hug him. The outstretched hands stopped. It was many days since he had bathed. The man standing opposite him was the epitome of cleanliness.

Basavappa laid his hands on Ayub's shoulders and laughed as if he could not believe himself. 'Where did you run away without telling anyone? How many years has it been? Where were you, what are you doing?'

Ayub's eyes dimmed with tears. 'Did you even recognize me? I am amazed. I cannot recognize you. You have become very fat.'

Basavappa burst out laughing. 'This is what happens when you eat dosa every day. You look like a scarecrow. Your face is unchanged but slightly older. What happened? Why didn't you even write a letter? These days, even the rickshaw man and those who launder our clothes have cell phones. Why are you like this?'

'That is a story, Basavappa. A horrifying story. Maybe you will believe it. Maybe you won't. But after hearing it, you will not even touch or speak to me.'

Basavappa looked at him thoughtfully. 'Did you think I might have changed? Will the mind change like our appearance does? Can I forget our friendship?' He laughed and sang '*Janda ooncha rahe hamara*', beating the table in rhythm.

Ayub laughed, nodding his head. Something rose like a ball from the pit of his stomach and constricted his throat. 'Basavappa, would you believe it if I say I get tears in my eyes every time I hear this song?'

'Definitely. I feel that way too. My kids think I'm crazy.'

Tiffin and coffee arrived.

'Why don't you eat too?' Ayub asked Basavappa.

'The first offering here is for me. This is my hotel. Is dosa enough? Eat idlis too. Hey, this man is our guest,' Basavappa replied.

Ayub's stomach was full. He had even forgotten all these tastes.

'Now tell me your story.'

Ayub felt embarrassed. 'First let me go home, Basavaa.'

'Ok, go home. Your mother will be happy. Poor thing, how she cried. She thinks you are dead, but I refused to believe that. Thank God you are alive. Why did you run away like that? Doesn't anyone else fail in their exams? Don't their parents scold them?'

Ayub bowed his head. He had forgotten his father's angry face, his spanking and his own anger long ago. 'Yes, I made a great mistake, Basavaa. Do you believe in fate?'

Basavappa looked at him steadily. 'If you had stayed here, fate could not have done anything to you. Come on, I'll walk with you until you reach home. Let us catch up as we walk.'

'Not now, Basavaa. I will tell you another day.'

'As you wish. You need not tell me anything. I'm so happy to see you. I am going to open a hotel in Srirangapatnam. Tipu Sultan's town. So I am going to call it Tipu's Café.' He winked and laughed. 'I need someone to help me. You can supervise it. Now look here, you should not keep crying so often.' Basavappa patted his back. 'Let's meet this evening.

Let's go to the Krishnaraja Sagar dam. There's been a lot of rain this year. So there's a lot of water there. Will look amazing,' he said.

Ayub smiled, nodded his head, and walked towards his house. His felt at ease. He could not believe that Basavappa had never changed. What would he say if he knew my story?

'You need not tell me anything.'

How come? Hadn't anything changed around here?

The streets were the same. He could not yet see any multi-storey buildings like in Mumbai. There were no glittering malls. Mysore was at peace, as if meditating on itself. The street he lived. The dusty ground in which he had played till he was 16 years old. The place where he had played cricket. The school he had studied in with Basavappa was in the next street. His father had not sent Ayub and his elder brother to the Madrasa school. 'You should study in the same school as other Indian children. We are not different. Education is your weapon,' he would say. 'Are you going to live your life selling flowers like your illiterate father?' he had asked on the day he beat Ayub, but Ayub did not feel like it was below his dignity to sell flowers. He could see Gulabi only there.

His feet halted abruptly. His house. Vappa and Ahmad would have gone to the flower shop. He stood outside the front door and pressed the bell.

'Who is it?' an old lady asked as she came to the door. His throat constricted. His eyes flooded. Her hair was white, her eyes dull.

'Ammi!' he said in a low voice.

She was shocked. She stared at him for a while. 'Who? Ayub? Have you returned?' she said and wept as she hugged him. 'I knew you would return one day. That you were alive. I was so angry because you were the stone-hearted boy who rejected us all and left.'

He broke down. Her warm embrace was cathartic, his tears washing away all the sorrow and humiliations of the past decades. He wept as if his heart would break. He was unable to speak.

'Don't cry. Come in. You ran away in anger. Do you understand how we suffered these past 20 years, not knowing if you were alive or dead? Did you remember home only now, all of a sudden?'

He shook his head firmly. He wiped his face and composed himself.

'There was never a minute when I didn't think of you these past 20 years. You must believe me.'

'Couldn't you call or write a letter?'

'I couldn't. I was the victim of a strange situation, Ammi. It is a horrifying story.'

His mother's eyes widened in fear. 'Did you do something wrong like some other idiot boys that would spoil our name? If so, leave immediately before Vappa returns.'

He was stunned at her intense expression. 'No, no. You must believe what I say.'

'Come in and tell me.'

The hall was dim as always. They both sat down on the old sofa there. Amma-*jaan* looked at him with tenderness.

She stroked his jaws. He felt despair when he saw tears flowing from her eyes. He wanted to dissolve his sorrows by hugging her.

'Did you have breakfast, my dear? Do you want coffee? Let me bring some,' she said getting up. He stopped her.

'No need, Ammi. I just had my breakfast.'

He grasped her hands. 'Ammi, every word I say is the truth. I will never lie.'

'Tell me. My daughter-in-law has gone to have her bath. There is no one at home."

'Ammi, can I lie down on your lap?'

'Yes dear.'

Her thigh felt like a cushion. Its soft warmth seemed to heal all his wounds. It seemed that he had lived for this very moment, waiting for it. He closed his eyes. He felt like a fourteen-year-old again.

How it rained that day! Ayub was lying on his bed in intense thought. He was unreasonably angry. Didn't anyone fail their exams? Should he have been beaten so brutally for that? He was sad that he had failed but even sadder that Vappa, who had never laid a hand on him, had belted him, and humiliated him with awful words. He found that unbearable. It created an unreasonable rage against Vappa. The place where Vappa had whipped him on the back stung like fire. Vappa had angrily pushed Ammi away when she had approached Ayub with some soothing balm. Everyone went to sleep that night as if nothing had happened. He could not sleep. He could not even cry through his anger. It was raining heavily outside.

He left after everyone was asleep. He had to go somewhere without telling anyone. Not even Basavaa. He would let Basavaa know later. He ran blindly, getting drenched in the rain.

He boarded a train in the station. He felt a strange freedom and agitation when it started moving. He had never gone anywhere alone. He had no money. He had never even thought about what his plans were. He hid from the ticket collector in the lavatory. He got down in the final stop. In Dadar, Mumbai. He had heard that Mumbai was a huge city. He would survive doing some job here. He only knew how to string flowers. What job would he get as a person who had failed his tenth standard? He was hungry.

He saw a jewellery shop. Ayub showed his gold ring to the person at the counter and told him he wished to sell it. Ayub had seen the white cap on the shopkeeper's head and realized he was a Muslim. So, he spoke to him in Urdu.

The shopkeeper looked at him keenly. 'Did you run away from home?' he asked.

Ayub lowered his head without replying.

'What is your name?'

'Ayub Khan.'

The shopkeeper weighed the ring, counted the money, put it in an envelope, and gave it to him. 'Keep it carefully. Mumbai is a dangerous place. Where are you going to stay?'

Ayub looked bewildered.

The shopkeeper smiled and took a woven white cap from a nearby shelf.

'Wear this on your head. You must not wander around without anything to identify you as a Muslim.'

He waited until Ayub had donned the cap. The boy wore it. In Mysore, he wore it only when he went to the mosque.

'You are my boy from now on. You can stay and eat in my house.'

Ayub was disbelieving. How many good people lived in Mumbai! He felt that reaching this place signalled a victory in some way. He would write to Ammi soon.

'Please let Vappa know that I am very happy here. I will soon earn on my own and show that I can become a big man.'

Yasin Mubarak seemed to be someone respected by all in that locality. There were four other boys like Ayub in his house. They spoke to Ayub kindly. He got three meals a day. They prayed five times a day. More than 50 people gathered during prayer time. He did his errands cheerfully.

Ayub had never expected to get such an easy life in a strange town and his heart filled with gratitude. He was wonderstruck at how good Yasin Mubarak, the man everyone called *Bade Bhai* (elder brother), was.

That day dawned as usual. Yasin Mubarak had risen early and was talking continuously on the phone with various people. In a change to the usual routine, Ayub was alone during prayer time.

The women of the house had disappeared. He was told that they had gone out of town. Breakfast came from a hotel. Yasin Mubarak did not go to his shop that day. Bhai had sent away everyone except Ayub and was sitting in front of the television.

News started trickling in. There had been blasts in several places in Mumbai. Ayub gasped as he watched from a corner. People died. Panicked crowds scattered, screaming. The hurt wailed. TV reporters were shouting in loud, anxious voices. He could not understand what they were saying. He froze in terror. He heard '*Aatankwadi* attacks' repeated several times. 'What is the meaning of *Aatankwadi*?' he asked in a loud voice.

Yasin Mubarak looked at him, startled. 'It means terrorists,' he said, slightly irritated.

'They are murderers. Devils. Why should they kill innocent people on the street? Are they our enemies? Are they Pakistanis?' Ayub asked, agitated.

'Shut up. Don't talk like a big man. Go do your errands,' said Mubarak with an anger Ayub had never seen before.

He got up and went to the room allocated to him. His heart was still beating in fear. What was happening in this city? He had never seen anything like it in Mysore. It was surprising that Bade Bhai had not gone to work today.

He wanted to bid farewell to Bade Bhai and leave for Mysore as soon as things calmed down. The street seemed deserted outside his window. Everyone was locked inside in fear. They stayed at home for the next two days. Bade Bhai did not go to his shop since the entire market street was closed. He seemed ready to leave for some place on the third day. The police came when he was trying to slip away through the back door.

Ayub was stunned. They pushed him and the other boys by the nape of their necks into a police van, even while he was observing these happenings with wide eyes. They were sent to jail straightaway. The crime he had committed and the reason he had been in jail remained a mystery to Ayub. He spent 20 years in isolation, unaware of what was going on in the outside world. The horrors he had experienced during that time…

He stopped. He could not bring himself to tell her the atrocities he had suffered. The beatings, kicking, and electric shock to his privates. The sexual perversities of guards and fellow prisoners. How could he tell all this to his mother?

"Ammi, I cannot describe to you what it was, the last twenty years. I suffered very much without understanding why. The day before, out of the blue, I was told that the court had decided that I was free and not guilty.'

'Did it take them 20 years to say that?' his mother asked, her eyes brimming with tears. She was silent for a long time, as if in deep thought. The warmth of her body made him sleepy. He felt relieved after having unburdened himself to her.

'Ayub, tell me the truth,' said Ammi softly. 'You didn't do anything wrong, did you?'

He was traumatized and got up with a start. 'Ammi, don't you believe in me? I told you the truth, Ammi.'

Ammi's eyes were full. It was obvious that she found it difficult to speak. She spoke without meeting his eyes, looking into the distance. 'Times are not good, Ayub. Many among our people are not even aware of what their kids are doing. Others look at us with suspicion if we even utter our name. We die with fear every time there is a blast in this country. Children disappear. Vappa will die of humiliation if the police ever come to our house.'

He looked at her, stricken. He seemed to see new worry lines in her face, already wrinkled and aged beyond her years. They seemed to increase like a netted web, transforming her face. He wanted to tear them away in his panic. How? On what should he swear to make her believe him? His stomach trembled. A nameless fear and confusion engulfed him. It was unbearable to recognize that Ammi would never believe him even if he explained it to her several times or swore on the holy Quran.

'Ammi,' he started, but she covered his mouth and grasped his hands.

'Ayub, please don't misunderstand me. Please go somewhere else, make a living, and survive. But please don't come back here,' she said in a low, furtive voice with tears in her eyes.

He stood looking at her in disbelief. Panic seemed to be compressing her. Ammi, it appeared, was waiting for him to leave quickly. Words came exploding from within him. 'Even the court has declared me innocent. I want to live a normal life too, Ammi. I want to work. I want to marry a girl I like. I will help father and support Ahmad. I have been waiting 20 years for this moment.'

'You leave, dear. If my daughter-in-law Gulabi knows, she will make a scene,' Ammi said, as he was wondering whether to say all this to her.

He was stunned and taken aback. 'Who?'

'Gulabi. She used to come to the flower shop. Ahmad liked her. They got married 10 years ago.'

Ayub took a few seconds to absorb what he had heard. The dream castles he had built crumbled in front of his eyes. They scattered into infinite pieces that could not be scooped up and blocked his heart.

It seemed like Ammi had been buried among those pieces. After a few seconds, he reverently placed her hands against his eyes and smiled slowly. He felt like there had never been a more insane person than himself. 'I'm going, Ammi,' he said and walked away without looking back.

His mind was blank. He walked to the bus terminus, stupefied. He quickly walked past Basavappa's hotel, boarded a bus at the terminal and sat near the window. The wind blew strong and cool. Dried leaves danced lightly above the ground, as if to signal that it was going to rain.

Original Tamil title: *Idaiveli*

Translated by Sukanya Venkataraman

# Hands

Savitramma[1] was startled. 'Does she mean me?' she thought, wondering if she should get up from her chair. 'Come on! Come on!' called the girl, even while she was processing that thought. Savitramma felt embarrassed, as if the whole world had heard that, because the girl had a microphone in her hand. Confused, she looked at Seshagiri Rao who was sitting next to her. 'Not alone, aunty! Bring him too, just a game aunty,' called the girl loudly, in a tone that the whole world could hear.

Seshagiri Rao held on to the arm of his chair and rose before she could offer her hand. His back was hunched like a 'C', with his shirt bunched up higher on his back. While she was considering if she should pull it down, he walked forward leaning on his cane. She walked with him, worried that he might stagger on his weak legs.

'Does this girl need to yell this over a microphone too,' wondered Savitri. Two couples were already standing there.

1 The protagonist of this story is Savitri. In South India, the suffix 'amma' is included as a mark of respect for older women or when respectfully addressing a woman who is higher in social status or wealth.

They were younger couples, she surmised. Husbands were standing close to their wives, as if ready for the 'game'. Only, Savitri didn't understand what that game was. When she stood next to Seshagiri Rao, the girl started questioning the first couple.

'How long have you been married?'

'Twenty-five years!'

'Wow!' said the girl, amazed. 'Do you fight?'

'A lot!'

'Yet you are together!'

The crowd laughed. 'There is no other option!' said the wife and the crowd laughed again.

The second couple had been married for thirty-five years. The girl went into raptures again. 'How are you living with the same man, aunty?'

'Unfortunately, I couldn't get a better man!' laughed the wife.

How could these women speak without any shame in a public place, Savitramma wondered.

'Tell me Sir, how long have you been married?'

'Fifty-nine! Sixty years in January!' responded Seshagiri Rao with pride sounding majestic, although he could not lift his back.

'Wow!' the girl gaped. She looked at the crowd. 'I can't believe it!' she said into her microphone.

The crowd applauded.

Savitramma was confused. No one had made her stand with her husband, made them the centre of attraction, and congratulated her for something that she never thought needed praise. She could not comprehend if this were praise or mockery. Seshagiri Rao may have felt the same way too. She felt she had been made a fool of because that girl treated them like they were from another planet. While she was considering returning to her chair, the girl—Champa seemed to be her name—said, 'Wait Sir. We are now going to test the depths of affection for your wife.'

Now what?

'We will blindfold you. Three women will stand in front of you, including your wife. You need to touch their hands and identify your wife.'

The crowd clapped in glee. Savitramma was convinced that they were indeed mocking her. Her son and daughter-in-law had forced her to come to this event. She did not even know where they were seated now. Was this even a game? Why torture a weak 85-year-old man? In addition, he had to touch strange women! And the crowd celebrates this. She felt sorry for her husband. His eyes were weak, unlike the past. Four young men tied his eyes with a black cloth. They held his hand and walked him forward.

Savitramma felt something stir inside her. A curtain rose, to tell her a tale of yore. A decorated four-seater carriage stood in front of her. The horse neighed, pawing the ground with its front legs but there was no sound. Like a scene from a silent movie. A tall, fair youth stood in front of her wearing a turban with decorative zari. Four others walked him forward, as if he didn't know how to walk.

'Why did four people hold and walk you forward?' she had asked him several years later. 'They were afraid I would run away. I was not interested in getting married!'

I wasn't interested either, she wanted to retort. Instead, she had remained silent. As a girl, she had been used to wearing a *langa*.[2] Now they had dressed her up in a heavy Dharmavaram[3] silk sari. It weighed her down as if made of iron. A plethora of flowers and *raakodi*[4] had been used to decorate her hair. It was painful. She wondered why she had to go through this discomfort and felt tearful. He came with music and pomp, surrounded by a noisy crowd. 'Hey Savitri, the boy looks like the Mysore Maharaja!' exclaimed her aunt.

'But he's thin,' aunt laughed, remembering the plump Maharaja who could not fit in the elephant's *ambaari*.[5]

'Is he on an elephant?' asked Savitri, her eyes wide and forgetting the pain momentarily.

'What wishful thinking!' Her aunt laughed again. 'This is a *jutka*, (single horse-carriage) Maharaja. Moreover, four people are holding him.'

'Check if he can walk properly!' exclaimed another aunt from Madhugiri.[6]

'I don't want this marriage,' said Savitri.

Four people were propelling Seshagiri Rao forward.

---

2 *langa*: skirt worn till the ankle by young girls in southern India.

3 Dharmavaram: A town in southern India known for manufacturing silk saris.

4 *Raakodi*: A round hair ornament worn by brides in southern India.

5 *Ambaari*: A canopied seat with elaborate decorations placed on an elephant's back, traditionally used by Indian royalty.

6 Madhugiri: A town in the southern state of Karnataka, India.

There was a lovely tulsi—holy basil[7]—plant in the backyard in a big, red cement planter that had lovely sketches on all four sides. Savitramma walked around it, watered the plant, muttered slokas, and moved on to her next round. She felt more tired today than usual. She couldn't get the words of the sloka right. It seemed like the girl was still calling out with her mike. The sound of applause and music still reverberated in her ears. Yesterday's gathering had tired her. She could not sleep last night.

It was hot too. It had never been this warm in Bengaluru at the end of May. Earlier, floors had been made of mud. One did not feel the heat when one walked on those floors made wet with a mixture of water and cow dung. Now floors were made of cement. They came in all colours and looked good but they felt hot. Even the holy tulsi plant was new. It had been bought in Lal Bagh. Everything had changed, like humans had changed. Even I have changed. I am not who I was yesterday. Circumambulating the planter and the tulsi are permanent fixtures, however, though new. She believed that some things remained the same, although appearances could change. Now, a question arose if there was any concept of permanency at all. The question staggered her because she was not used to questioning. Her mind went round and round like a bull in an oil press. It came back and stood in the same place, as if in search of something she had lost.

7 *Tulsi:* The holy basil or *tulsi* plant is considered sacred in Hinduism.

Savitramma stood holding the side of the planter. A sudden question arose in her mind on why she was circling this plant ever since she remembered.

Her legs were used to this, even as a naked child with her mother Gangamma. She used to say that holy basil was a woman like us. The healthy plant had withered suddenly before her father's death. He had never had a day's sickness in his life. When he was brought back by others as a corpse, after having gone to work in the field that morning, her mother wept holding the holy basil plant, 'Was this the news you were conveying?' Savitramma had remembered that for a long time.

Looking back, it seemed like her mother had lived in the *Treta Yuga*.[8] Plants, birds, and the Gods had been friends with each other then. They had conveyed messages in their secret language. Now, there was a scientific explanation if a plant wilted: too much water, the root has rotted. There were psychological and logical explanations even if the human mind changed. Her daughter's son had been to the United States to study this.

Savitramma felt like she had one leg in the Treta Yuga and one in the present age. People might laugh if she bestowed divine properties on a mere holy basil plant, like her mother had. She completed her final round of the plant and went to the backyard. She bent over to scoop some water with a

---

8 *Treta Yuga*: A Sanskrit word denoting the second of the four yugas, or ages of mankind in Hinduism. It is said to have lasted 3,600 divine years, or 1,296,000 human years. According to Hinduism, we now live in the Kali Yuga, the fourth and last age of mankind.

small metal container in the water tank next to the well. The blue sky had descended in the still water. She saw her face looking back at her.

The white silk of her hair wavered like dissipating white clouds in the water. The big kumkum dot on her forehead seemed intent on turning attention away from the many wrinkles on her face. She looked at her face and the sky behind it for a while as if worrying that her reflection would scatter if she touched the water with the little metal jug. The hand holding the jug had prominent veins, crisscrossed with wrinkles. There were green and red bangles on the wrist. She had worn them without question since her mother had insisted that *sumangalis*[9] had to wear them.

When she plunged the jug into the water, her face disintegrated like a *rangoli*[10] in water. The clouds dispersed. The hand seemed uglier and more wrinkled in the water. It seemed like the lines of age had taken over from top to bottom, like an accident that had happened without her knowledge. Perhaps some corner of her inner self had been dissociated and detached from that fact. It was sitting there, still a little girl wearing a skirt. Was that possible? Yesterday, that girl Champa had dragged that child out into the open. Savitramma thought she should never have permitted that intrusion into her space. She felt sad, like she had been made a fool of. She thought she could not share it with anyone.

---

9 *Sumangalis*: A Tamil word denoting a married woman.

10 *Rangoli*: Geometrical or floral elaborate patterns drawn with rice powder by women, usually at the entrance of Hindu households, in southern India.

Today, she felt like some emotions and feelings were hers alone. Others might laugh them off as trivial if she shared them, but these emotions were the result of her very roots being shaken. Maybe this thought would not have arisen if she hadn't gone to that event, but that remained unclear. In fact, she felt that her confusion had increased. Her eyes had been blindfolded and she had walked around like Gandhari.[11] Darkness still encompassed her. Yet, she needed light to understand it.

As a rule, she was not one to voice her thoughts. Perhaps it was because she may not have had any thought worthy of sharing. There was no connection between her world and Seshagiri Rao's. She had not even wished for that connection. She wondered if that had been a mistake but there had been a wall in between. The other men and women of the house consented to that, as if it were a universally acknowledged rule.

She felt his kingdom was not one she could enter nor understood her panic when she considered it. He had made her believe that there was no need for her to know about his professional world. Perhaps because of his certain belief that she neither had the standing or intelligence to comprehend his world. He may have thought that there was no need for her to understand him in entirety. There would have been many secret rooms in his world, she knew. She now

---

11 Gandhari: An important character in the Indian epic *Mahabharata*. She was a princess of Gandhara and the wife of Dhritrashtra, the blind king of Hastinapura, and the mother of a hundred sons, the Kauravas. She blindfolded herself as a mark of devotion to her husband who had been born blind.

understood that he had not been interested in knowing her fully either.

It seemed like there had been more lust than affection when he made love in the dark, after the lights had been switched off. She felt acutely embarrassed when she remembered how she had yearned for his fierce touch, mistakenly deluding it for love. That led to eight children. Nurturing them into good adults and completing 59 years of married life didn't seem like a huge achievement. Her life had moved forward on its own. Like a dry leaf floating on a river current.

She had seen her sons and daughters live different lives. She was amazed when her daughter-in-law spoke knowledgeably about her son's business, as if running it. It was not possible to narrow this relationship because they were educated.

New questions arose today. What does he know about me? Do I know him fully? Her ignorance scared her, like an orphan standing at the crossroads.

'*Ajji! Ajji!*'[12]

She retrieved her hand which was stroking the water. She looked up, wiping her wet hand.

Her granddaughter Lavanya was standing on the steps leading into the backyard.

'What are you doing, *Ajji*? You were away for a long time.'

'I was saying my prayers to the tulsi. It was delayed today because my bath was delayed. Is there anything you wanted to share?'

---

12 *Ajji*: Grandma, in the Kannada language.

Lavanya descended the steps and grasped Savitramma's hand to support her while negotiating the steps.

'Well, dad, uncle and grandpa have all eaten. Come and eat. Aren't you hungry?'

'No. I don't feel good after eating out yesterday. I will be fine if I skip a meal.'

'Please eat at least rasam and rice, grandma!'

'Alright.'

Lavanya laughed. 'Seems like you ate a lot at the party yesterday. Grandpa is fine. He ate as usual.'

'He is used to eating out!'

'Did he never take you out to eat?'

'No. That was not the norm in those days.'

'If my husband eats out without me, I will not spare him!' said Lavanya, laughing again. 'Poor grandma! Haven't you ever been angry with grandpa?'

Savitramma smiled and shook her head saying 'no'.

'That is why grandpa still hassles you.'

'Lavanya, please keep quiet!' scolded Kamala, her mother and Savitramma's daughter-in-law. Lavanya ran in on hearing the telephone ring, glad to use it as an excuse to leave.

While eating, her three daughters-in-law were quiet. This was unusual, noted Savitramma. God knows what Kamala had told them. In the hall, Lavanya was talking enthusiastically into the telephone.

'Oh, listen! Even my grandma and grandpa went to the Senior Citizen's Club event. My elder uncle and aunt persuaded them to attend. It seems grandma and grandpa even played games. They had a great time.'

Savitramma cast an appealing look at her daughters-in-law.

'Let it be, *Amma* (mother). Lavanya cannot be restrained,' said Kamala.

The others continued eating with a smile. Perhaps it was mockery, concluded Savitramma. It indicated that the news would be heard by all their relatives. There was no point talking about it anymore. Savitramma ate and thankfully went to the room she shared with her husband. Seshagiri Rao was lying at one end of the double bed placed in the middle of the room, facing the window. His curved back seemed even more curved.

She could not recall when he had started developing a hunch. She wanted to caress it once she perceived it, but knew he disliked it. He had even refused to take medical help for his hunch. Aware that he would wake up at the least noise, she closed the door quietly and lay down on her back on the other side of the bed. They shared the same bed even after begetting grandchildren, but he had never turned to her. He always slept facing the window. She had even felt that his hunch would become better if he lay on his back like her.

Savitramma felt sleepy because she had slept badly the previous night. Sleep was scattered, however. The sound of music and applause bored into her head like a beetle. Everyone was dancing. Singing, dancing, and clapping. Not praising Lord Krishna or Rama. They were singing something called rock music, which was played from a record. Everyone was over 60.

The song celebrated life. Savitramma felt like dancing too. She had never felt as light in her life. Thoughts about Seshagiri Rao did not pursue her. 'Sing, sing. Dance, dance…' The girl Champa was commanding them like a circus ring master.

Seshagiri Rao started singing out of the blue… '*Namma Thippar halli balu thoora!*'[13] (Our village Thippar is very far away). He used to sing this song when they were newly married. Did he still remember it?

'Come here, Sir! Come and identify your wife!'

Savitramma felt sorry for him. He, blindfolded, touched the hand of every woman. The first lady was younger. A friend of Champa. She had smooth hands. Seshagiri Rao moved to the next woman. The second lady could have been around 60. She felt at peace when her husband moved away, towards her. 'Yes, it is me. It is me,' she wanted to exclaim. He touched her hands for a few seconds and said, 'No, not this one'. She felt like she had been slapped when he moved on. He went back to the first girl. 'This is my wife!' he declared.

'Oh God,' muttered Savitramma.

Someone touched her hand. She turned, startled. Seshagiri Rao was now lying down facing her. She looked at him disbelievingly. He held her hand high and studied it. 'When did your hands become so rough?' he asked. 'They used

13 A Kannada song celebrating one's native village.

to be as soft and delicate as a jasmine flower. That is what I remember, Savitri!'

She felt like crying. 'Have you forgotten that I've become older too? You have a hunch now. Will my hands not become rough?'

'I only remember your petal-soft hands,' he said with a small laugh. He caressed her hand for a while. 'Why don't you apply some oil on it?' he asked.

She wanted to laugh. She felt like she could never share her feelings about this moment with anyone. Not even with this silly old man.

Original Tamil title: *Marathi.*
Translated by: Sukanya Venkataraman

# The Steering Wheel

The car sped along its familiar route. She wondered if she even needed to place her hand on the steering wheel. The car seemed to come alive and move by itself once she sat in it and opened the garage door. Strange. Who would believe it, if someone said that a car had a soul and emotions of its own? It seemed weary when she was tired. It simply would not start then. Once on the road, though, it never stopped half-way through. It would wait until she reached home. Then it would heave a sigh and give up, as if asking her to leave it alone. She would text her mechanic David. His phone was always on silent mode and he only read messages. He would come by to repair her car, muttering under his breath. 'Why on earth are you still driving a car that needs to be trashed?'

She would never respond. He would laugh if she told him that her car had a soul. It bore the burden of her memories, both good and bad. Sitting inside it was like sitting with a friend—a friend who knew her most intimate self. But David would not understand. No one knew the tears she had shed in that car, her head buried in its steering wheel. It had been cathartic to weep into it without restraint. Its silence seemed like a friend's embrace.

Memories raced through her today as she gripped the steering wheel. She could not fathom why. Then she saw the date and time on the car's clock. Ohhhh…her mind trembled. Her forehead and palms warmed up. She started sweating. The force of that memory still terrified her. Initially, it was with her all the time, everywhere, tormenting her. Familiar and strange voices—their anger, curses, and sorrow…that anger! It seemed like the whole world was angry. It was unbearable. It made her panic. It seemed like the world had gathered, fingers pointing at her. This is the woman. This is she. They were unaware that she was one of them and part of that crowd. They did not know how it isolated, humiliated and made her the guilty person. The questions of how and why, along with her role in it, were like whiplashes. That was the past now. An old story; a story that transformed her path. This car had played a key role in guiding her then. She had even given it a name. Dolly. She never questioned why she had chosen that name.

'I have named my car Dolly.'

'It is my doll.'

'My car is my doll, darling.'

'No!'

She wanted to laugh at that show of anger. What else could she do in the face of a three-year-old's temper? She never changed that name. Dolly…my Dolly. What did it all go wrong? How did it start? What is right and what is wrong?

Who could explain that to her? The car seemed to move forward of its own volition.

She followed its path anxiously with many questions. I don't understand Dolly…how could I have been so stupid? 'Mere intelligence isn't enough Maggie. We lack foresight,' George had said. All I know is that the world went dark that day. I am a good person, Dolly. I have never done anything wrong. I went to church every Sunday. Even now, to confess; although I don't comprehend what I should beg forgiveness for. My voice quivers. I want to cry…yes, even now…'

'Margita!...Margita…!'

Margarita woke up with a start. Lara clapped and laughed as if revelling in waking her up. Margarita felt like she was still holding the steering wheel. She rubbed her palms together firmly. Lara was drooling. Margarita gently wiped her mouth with a tissue. Lara touched her cheek.

'What baby?'

'Are you okay?' Only Margarita could understand Lara's slurred words.

'I'm fine baby. Margita is an old woman, right? So she falls asleep at odd times.'

'Margarita is not an old woman.'

Margarita wanted to laugh. 'Thank you, baby. Shall we go to the park after tea?'

Lara laughed happily. 'Let's.'

Margarita prepared tea in the kitchen and placed it along with Lara's favourite cookies on the table in front of Lara's wheelchair. She broke a cookie and fed it to Lara, in between sips of tea. She was drinking her tea when Lara unexpectedly kissed her forearm and said, 'I love you'. Margarita felt a thrill run through her body.

Lara said it often these days at the most unexpected moment. 'I love you too, Lara,' replied Margarita.

'I love you,' repeated Lara when Margarita kissed her forehead. As if there was some difference in how they loved each other. 'Park, park!' shouted Lara as soon as she had eaten the cookies.

Margarita hurriedly cleaned their cups in the kitchen and got Lara ready with a sweater and a cap. 'We can go now,' she said, smiling, Lara loved going out. Especially, to the park. Today, thankfully, was a bright, sunny day. It was cherry blossom time. Flowers bloomed like an umbrella over the trees with their leaves hidden under. Lara was ecstatic at the sight and clapped her hands and laughed.

Habitual park goers waved to them and went on their way. Lara waved back. Margarita walked, pushing the wheelchair as always. This walk had been happening for more than 15 years. Every plant knew Lara and Margarita. In this interval, some walkers had disappeared. To others, this duo was an integral part of the park, to the extent of asking 'Why didn't you come?' if they were not at the park for even a day. She could not remember when the initial suspicion and surprise had evaporated. Those who had hesitated to smile earlier, now beamed in a friendly manner. They discussed the weather. Or asked after Lara.

It was harder to walk today. The weight of her memories seemed to weigh her down. After walking for a short while, she stopped near a bench. 'Lara, shall we sit here? I am feeling tired today,' she said.

Lara nodded, smiling vaguely. Margarita felt like resting. She leaned back on the bench and closed her eyes. Lara was content to sit in silence, looking around her.

Sleep seemed to overwhelm her as soon as she closed her eyes—the result of not sleeping last night. She shouldn't have watched television, especially the news bulletin. It seemed like such news was purposely broadcast to terrify her. Her heart quivered. It has happened somewhere in the distance, in some place in California. But it had felt like she was an eyewitness. So many wails…screams of the hurt. The police was busy removing bodies; pre-pubescent boys and girls. A couple, a husband and wife, the news said, had attacked. They were now dead too. She could clearly see the stunned crowd. Her eyes seemed to pop out of their sockets, her heart palpitating in horror. How? How could they do this? Was this treason? Treachery? Mental illness? Religious fanaticism? Maggie was now inside the television screen. She too was asking questions. Why? For what?

Maggie's closed eyes filled with tears. Those children… their parents…how would they cope? Her consciousness slipped away from her body into a chasm, into dark passages and crevices. 'Mom!' 'Mom!' The echoes reflected off the walls of an underground cave and slammed into her. She started running in panic. 'No. Go away. Disappear. I don't know you…Don't call me. Go…' Still, the voices chased her. 'Mom!...Mom!' An army of children's voices. 'The mistake is yours…You are the murderess. Catch her…catch Maggie…'

She looked around her with dread. She was in a strange place. She could not find her plants. There were no roses… no colours. It was dark and empty. There was a crowd around her with strange, hateful stares. She tried to hide her face when George hugged her and cried as if her heart would break. How? Why? What was my mistake? George patted her back silently. 'I don't know either, Maggie. I don't understand it either…' Tears exploded from deep inside her.

'Margita! Margita!'

She woke up with a start. Her cheeks were wet. Lara was gazing at her. 'Don't cry,' she said, extending her hand. Overcome with emotion,

Margarita grasped Lara's hands. 'Will you forgive me Lara?' she asked.

Lara gave a guileless smile and then looked confused. 'I don't know,' she said. 'Don't cry'. She wiped Margarita's face with a tissue.

Margarita gathered herself. 'Sorry baby,' she said. What a fool I am.

'I don't know.' Did Lara understand what she was saying? Margarita shook her head as if to rid herself of that thought. No. 'I am going crazy,' she mumbled to herself. The park was getting more crowded. Dog walkers and returning office goers were coming in now. She knew Lara became agitated in crowds.

'Let's go home Lara," said Margarita. Lara did not respond. Margarita wondered why Lara was silent until they reached home. Had she confused the girl? 'I'm such a fool.' Dorothy and John had already returned from work when they reached the house.

'Hi Margarita,' Dorothy greeted her as usual. 'How was your walk in the park?' 'Hi baby,' she said to Lara.

'Hi,' replied Lara without enthusiasm. Then she carefully strung her words together and said slowly, 'Margita cried'.

Margarita was jolted. 'Oh no,' she began, but Lara interrupted with a loud, 'Yes, yes'.

Dorothy looked surprised. Then she came close to Margarita and sighed. 'Let it be. I understand,' she said softly.

Margarita recovered her composure. 'Sorry Lara. I will not cry again. I will be a good girl,' she said softly.

'OK' said Lara, shrugging her shoulders, which made Margarita smile.

'Tea is ready Maggie. Come and join me,' Dorothy said. Margarita switched on a television programme for Lara and sat next to Dorothy.

'Sorry Dorothy. I fell asleep on a park bench. A bad dream. I should not have watched the news on TV yesterday. I must have cried in my dream.'

'There is no need to explain yourself,' replied Dorothy. They sat quietly for some time, drinking tea and drowned in their own thoughts.

'Maggie, I need to tell you something. John and I never thought Lara would progress so much. You came into our lives like an angel!'

Margarita snapped her head up and said, 'Please Dorothy. Say no more.'

Dorothy looked at her keenly. 'Did you know that Lara is insightful? She has the capacity to somehow understand our emotional state.'

Margarita remained silent for a long time. She washed her cup. Then she took Lara to the restroom, dressed her in her nightclothes and put her to bed.

Lara caught Maggie's hand as she was leaving. 'Are you a good girl?' she asked.

Maggie's stomach flipped for no fathomable reason. 'I don't know Lara,' she said with a slow smile. 'I think I am a good girl'.

'Then don't cry.'

Margarita kissed Lara's hands. 'No. I will not cry'.

Lara closed her eyes without responding. 'I need to sleep,' she muttered.

Margarita shut the door softly and came out of the room. Dorothy was talking to someone on the phone. She sounded agitated. Ah, the terror incident in California. Maggie waved and indicated that she was leaving.

Dorothy's agitated voice and flustered face seemed to follow her as she got into her car. Panic gripped the depths of her stomach all over again. Oh God, why were the demons chasing her? What has happened to human beings? What do they want? There seemed to be a problem somewhere, but she did not know what it was.

The priests in her church did not comprehend either. 'No one has any hope now, Margarita,' Reverend Joseph had told her 15 years back. Thank God he wasn't alive today. How would he have explained yesterday's shooting that had killed 15 innocent lives who had assembled for some entertainment, in the name of God? Religious fanaticism or mental illness, there was hatred behind it all. Anger. No one knew the reason for this anger. Has man's basic nature changed? Are we born with anger? Or does it imprint itself on us later? What does that anger want to satiate? Can it ever be forgiven?

'I don't know.' Was it an indication that Lara understood what she had said? Or was it an innocent remark?

She recalled Dorothy's face again. And the anger reflected in her face. Maggie could understand that anger. She had seen Dorothy's true face today, after 15 years of acquaintance. It relaxed her, strangely. Looking back she has always been amazed that she had had the courage to meet Dorothy at all.

The day is vivid in her memory. Her usual bakery had been more crowded than it normally was. She had felt weary and 10 years older when she recalled the past week's events. She had slumped down in a corner bench and closed her eyes not wanting to listen to the chatter around.

'The doctor has confirmed that the child is brain damaged. He has advised Dorothy to look after the kid at home. But

John and Dorothy need to work to handle the medical expenses. Nurses are too expensive. How terrible! They were such a happy family. Who knew this would happen?'

'Well, we only know about Dorothy.'

'Only this child survived despite being hit. The other kids…'

She paid for the bread and returned to her car. She buried her head in the steering wheel and wept, her chest heaving. She wondered if she should go to George's office. He wouldn't like that.

'What should I do Dolly?'

Dolly was silent. Maggie took a deep breath and started the car, the words of those women churning inside her head. The car seemed to drive itself. She was startled when it stopped. Where am I? George had shown her this house once. He had been highly agitated then. 'No, no, let's leave before they see us,' he had said. They had obsessively checked on the girl's status with the hospital, as if crazed. How was the girl doing?

Her mind was in a daze now. The question of whether she should approach that house ever, did not arise. She reached the front door and pressed the bell. Dorothy opened the door after Maggie had pressed the bell twice. She looked shocked. Maggie started talking hurriedly before Dorothy could say a word.

'Please don't tell me to leave. Please provide me with an opportunity to help you. I will take care of Lara. I have worked as a nurse.'

Dorothy seemed stunned. 'But...'

'I don't want a salary. Please believe me. You can check with Reverend Joseph about me...You can then call me.'

George waited along with her for the call... It came after two days.

---

The vehicle's clock indicated that it was seven o'clock. She realized she had not started the car yet to go home. 'Dolly, let's go,' she said, as if she expected it to reply. The car drove itself, as always, to reach the house. Lost in her thoughts, she entered the garage, locked the car, and went into her house. She vowed not to go near the TV that evening. She took her simple dinner from the fridge, heated it, and ate. She then took a book with her to bed.

Her eyes refused to focus on the book. Her mind whirled. A deep sense of loneliness enveloped her. The memory of George's non-descript death five years ago pained her. It would be wonderful if her end happened that way too. Before that, though, she needed to release the burden weighing her down. It was a restless night hovering between sleep and wakefulness, between dream and reality. Early next morning she woke with a start when Dorothy's call came.

'Lara developed a fever last night, Maggie. We had to admit her in a hospital.'

Maggie answered even before Dorothy finished: 'I'll come right away.'

She got ready in a panic. What happened to Lara? She had been fine the previous day. Dolly obediently deposited her at the hospital's entrance. Lara lay with her eyes closed, an oxygen tube connected to her nose. Dorothy looked relieved when she saw Maggie.

'She suddenly seemed breathless and we had to come here.'

'You did the right thing. Both of you can rest and return later. I will be here,' said Margarita.

'Thank you, Maggie. I don't know how to thank...'

'Shhh...now go.'

She felt disturbed when she saw Lara lying still with her eyes closed, her head shaking involuntarily. A 21-year-old young woman, with a brain that did not develop beyond that of a five-year-old child. Her Lara...who had survived because she had cared for her these last 15 years...A child, who did not realize that her body had changed into a woman. Dorothy had told her that Lara had the insight to understand others' deeper emotions. Could this be true?

The doctors kept testing Lara. 'Will she be alright?' Maggie asked them again and again. 'Will she recover?'

They did not respond. She stayed in Lara's room that night with the doctor's permission. She stroked Lara's hand with a single prayer. 'Give me a chance'. Would Lara understand? Lara, Lara...She bent down and buried her head on the rim of the bed, still holding Lara's hand and delving deep into the darkness, she cried.

She could see the morning light in the darkness. Tom was standing before her.

'Bye Mom!'

She still remembered his kiss. He had soft lips. He left to go somewhere. She said 'Bye' to his back. After George left for his office, she too left for the shop where she worked.

There was a school on her route. It was a happy and cheerful place with boys and girls in their white and blue uniforms. Tom had studied there too. It filled her heart with joy every time she passed that school. It offered a different sight today. It was crowded with people and vehicles. Then she saw the police. Many parents were there with worried expressions. She could hear screams. Some young girls were hugging each other and crying. Panicked, she stopped the car on the side of the road. She lowered her window. 'What's going on?' she asked a woman there.

'Some crazy man entered the school and started shooting.'

'God, was he caught?'

'The police shot him dead.'

'Oh my God!'

'The scoundrel. How many children…I counted eight bodies. Three children were taken to the hospital. Who knows if they will survive…' Bodies being transported into the ambulance, the blue uniforms now red…

Margarita sobbed, still holding Lara's hand. 'Lara, you were the only survivor, but a bullet damaged your brain.' Her fingers shook. 'Lara, that sinner was my son, Tom. He was a mild boy. I had no idea that a demon lived inside him. I couldn't understand it at all. I—his own mother. I have no idea where I went wrong…sorry…sorry…'

When she woke up the next morning, Lara was staring at her. Maggie felt deeply touched. She grasped Lara's hand. 'How are you baby?' she asked.

Lara gave her a deep look and said, 'Don't cry'.

'No, I won't cry.'

'Love you, Margita,' Laura said.

Did she hear me? Is she saying this with conscious understanding? Maggie wasn't sure. But she felt lighter, as if the weight inside her had lifted.

When she left for home that day, the steering wheel seemed especially easy to handle. She did not have the time to react when it came off in her hand. David, her mechanic, shook his head when he heard the news. 'I was always telling her to trash that car'.

Original Tamil title: *Steering Wheel*
Translated by: Sukanya Venkataraman

# Ganga's Choice

The movie poster was stuck to the terrace wall. It was the poster of *Kochadaiiyaan*, yet to be released. Rajinikanth seemed youthful in the poster. Ganga was wonderstruck. How does he get younger by the day? She was a big fan of the actor. Who else could impersonate his rakish look and his style of flinging a cigarette in the air and catching it with his mouth? She would be amused when Rajini clicked his finger and said '*En vazhi thani vazhi*' (My way is a unique way). Above all, she loved that Kannada accent in his Tamil. He was from Bengaluru after all. How else would he speak? Perhaps he had not cared to change it or he could only speak Tamil with a lisp, despite trying hard not to. Either way, it made her feel that Rajini was 'our guy' because she too spoke Tamil with a lisp like him. She did not like seeing his face today, though. She had never dreamt that it would become problematic.

'What kind of woman hangs the picture of an actor on the wall?' Until today, no one—not even her husband—had ever asked her that question.

'Why? What's wrong with that? I like him. What's your problem?' She had asked laughingly, as if it was a joke. 'Maybe that had been wrong,' she thought now.

'That won't work well if you want to be part of a respectable family.'

Ganga should have spat on his face then. Anger shot up from the pit of her stomach into her heart and strangled her throat. She wanted to cuss. She could only cuss in Kannada. *Soole mavanae*[1]...*lopar*[2]...She got up abruptly and began to tear the poster. It wasn't easy to tear a poster stuck with glue made from *maida* (refined flour). Poor Rajini looked pathetic with his mouth and ears torn. She stared at him with rising irritation for a while and walked away. 'Let it be. Why should I tear this poster because of what that man said? I'll stick another one tomorrow. What could anyone do anyway?'

'*Lopar*...Hey, that's not "*lopar*" but "loafer,"' laughed the mistress of the house she worked in.

'That's how we say it, Ma'am,' she had answered. *Lopar*... some bad word. *Lopar*...*lopar*...

Tiger knew to let her be when Ganga was angry. She was now sitting on the ground leaning against the wall and scolding someone. Tiger raised his head slightly to look at her and lowered it again. Let her scold. It even felt happy when she scolded someone. Meaningless words were pouring from her mouth like pebbles and hail clattering to

1 *Soole mavanae:* A cuss word in Kannada (son of a bitch).

2 'Loafer' was pronounced '*lopar*' by Ganga.

the ground. There was a rhythm to that. It was even relaxing to listen with closed eyes.

The mobile phone rang and trilled a Kannada movie song. A favourite of Ganga's. She let it sing. 'Let anyone call,' she thought indifferently. It might be the lady from No. 12. She hadn't gone to work there yesterday. She hadn't gone today either because of her mental turmoil since morning. The phone rang for a long time and stopped. Tiger looked at her as if asking why she hadn't taken the call. 'I'm not talking to anyone today, including you,' Ganga said. Tiger gave up and closed his eyes.

The song started again. She took the call after a delay. It was No. 12.

'I'm unwell, Ma'am.'

'What's wrong?'

'I have a fever.'

'Couldn't you call and let me know you were unable to come in today? Why do you have a mobile otherwise?'

'I couldn't even open my eyes. There isn't even anyone to make me a cup of tea,' Ganga said, suppressing her irritation. Her words trembled. Sorrow constricted her throat as if she was talking about a death. She was the most unfortunate being ever, she thought, and felt like bursting into tears.

'All right, take care of yourself. You will come in tomorrow, right? The kitchen sink is full of unwashed dishes.'

'I'll be there, Ma'am.'

'People think only of their problems,' she said to Tiger. 'Ma'am is not bothered if Ganga has fever. 'Sink is full of dirty dishes!' she mimicked her mistress. 'Why don't you wash one day?' Tiger wagged his tail vigorously in agreement and moved closer to her. He sank his face into her thighs and closed his eyes.

'Will this dog be with you always?'

'Yes, he will.'

Who was this man? He and his awful stare.

Ganga held Tiger's forelegs and started dancing. A song was blaring. There was gentle snowfall. A yellow rose laughed from the pot. Ganga whirled round and round.

'I am different… Why shouldn't I be?'

'What arrogance? Shouldn't you be more modest? Do you know who they are?'

Tiger opened his eyes and looked for her. It seemed like he had been dreaming. Ganga was nowhere to be seen. He ran in hurriedly. Ganga had locked the door and left.

Today was hotter than yesterday. There was a flight of open steps leading into the street from the terrace. That was the advantage and disadvantage to her house. She could walk into the street without meeting anyone who lived downstairs but there was also the danger that any weirdo could come up and bash the door down. 'This seems dangerous. Let's not live here, Ganga,' Seeni had warned from the beginning.

She had insisted. 'Why should I be afraid when you are there for me?' she had asked and laughed. The terrace, the breeze and a distant view of the Madiwala Lake[3] reminded her of the balconies in the houses where she worked. She

3 Madiwala Lake: One of the biggest lakes in Benguluru, Karnataka.

could also have pots of flowers. There was plenty of space for the puppy to play in. The pup had come to her as if someone had beckoned it to her.

'Let's somehow lease it. It is so hard to pay rent every month.'

'We need to give two lakhs,' muttered Seeni.

'Why do I contribute to two chit funds? This is the time to withdraw that money. We will be fine for two years. After that, we can take the lease money back.'

She never allowed him to talk beyond that.

'What I say once is equal to saying it a hundred times,' she mimicked Rajini's dialogue. She finally got her wish. She had worked hard for 10 years to earn that money. Flowerpots sat close to the terrace walls. The rose saplings from the houses she worked in bloomed under her green thumb. Everyone seemed surprised. 'How come the rose plants are blooming so well at the touch of her hand?'

Those conceited women spoke within her hearing. 'Does she have so much money that she can afford to lease a house?' Such jealous creatures. She was convinced that she was suffering because of their curses.

Ganga still felt lousy as she descended the steps on to the street and saw three women with kids on their hips in the street corner chatting. They turned their faces away on seeing her. What on earth would they talk about? Ganga walked past them. She could sense that she was the subject of their talk.

'Look, some people refuse to accept good advice.'

'Sheer arrogance, what else?'

'And for no reason at all! Not even normal to claim a status.' They started giggling.

Ganga wanted to go back, catch them by their hair and fling them against the wall screaming, 'What is being normal? What is your status, you fools?'

She controlled herself. They would simply deny they were talking about her and mock her. She should not get into an argument with these creatures today. They each had a kid on their hip. Mallika was pregnant too. Her husband was a drunkard. He beat her every day. Why was this shameless ass sleeping with him? Disgusting. I call *that* abnormal. What stature does she have to mock me? The only stature she had was getting pregnant. They announced it all over. When Mallika came of age, her mother could not even afford a square meal. Yet, she had borrowed money here and there to organize a big lunch for everyone. She still struggles to repay her debts.

'What a grand lunch it was,' Ganga had remarked to her mother.

'That is the norm to inform everyone that a girl has come of age. Then people will approach the family to seek her hand in marriage,' her mother had said, without explaining the rest.

'Hey Kaliamma, when is your grand lunch?'

Kaliamma would click her tongue. 'Who knows what is written on her head? I don't understand. They say that some girls come of age late.'

Ganga went where her legs took her. A cool breeze was blowing. She could see the Madiwala Lake a short distance away. A man who looked like Seeni was standing on the bank. She felt a slight thrill. Her legs walked faster without her knowledge. It seemed like the lake moved backwards as she walked towards it. The man also moved. The lake was still when she stood on its banks. The man was nowhere to be seen. She sat on a mound. She had first seen Seeni here. It was here he had said he would marry her.

She still remembered how overwhelmed she had felt. She felt like the heroine of a Tamil film she had seen.

'Really?'

'Really. Would anyone lie about this?'

She could not believe his words. Her ears had been used to hearing remarks like '*Who on earth would marry you*?'

'Why are you silent, Ganga?'

'Do you know about me?'

'Yes.'

'What do you know?'

'Oh, they say all kinds of things. I don't want to know all that. I want you.'

Really? Really? The entire town asked. Even her mother asked.

Ganga looked at the still lake.

Was there a God? She felt there was no God. The women in the street said God existed. They conveyed their thanks by fasting. They walked on fire. They wore garlands and went to Melmaruvathur.[4] She had indulged in none of this.

4 Melmaruvathur: A famous pilgrimage town in Tamil Nadu with a temple dedicated to the Goddess Shakti (the feminine personification of primordial energy or force).

She thought that even if God did exist, He was a partial God. If God was just, would these women dare talk this way about her?

'Look, look. Look at the way she dresses. Who is she plotting to seduce?'

'She is confident she doesn't need to worry about getting pregnant no matter who she sleeps with.'

The voices would lower to a whisper. 'I even wonder if she is a woman at all.'

Initially, Ganga had felt angry and sad when she heard them gossip. She had felt inept to argue with them as equals. They were a gang. If someone said something about one of them, it was amazing how the whole town gathered in their support. In the end, she would lose. Their words had a terrifying impact. She would feel tremendously weary, as if she were lower than the lowest being in existence.

She had tried to drown herself twice in this lake. She was not even lucky enough to die. Someone had rescued her. When the neighbouring crowd came to check in on her, she had screamed like one possessed and chased them away.

She buried her head in her knees. Memories of Seeni raged inside her. She wanted to wail out loud. It seemed like his entry into her life had been a big lie. 'You are a fraud. A *Lopar*. Tiger did not eat well for a month. He had been lying at the entrance, waiting for you.'

She remembered how she too had waited like that. She felt a deep sorrow because she felt that a great injustice had been done to her. The women on her street said it was a miracle that he had lived with her for a year. She was clueless about how she could avenge their words.

She had been fine when alone, unaware what was wrong with her. She was keen to earn money. Her mother had drummed that into her head. 'You have to earn your own money. There is no guarantee that any man will want you.' Saving had become a necessity. She was able to dress well, even after saving. Her body might not have been as voluptuous as Mallika's but the mirror seemed to vouch for her pretty face. She became more aware of it when men standing in the street's tea shop stared at her. Seeni would tell her that she looked like a movie star when she wore fake *jimikkis*[5] and an artificial necklace.

They exchanged garlands in a Mariamman[6] temple nearby and got married. They did not organize a big lunch for the community. It appeared that the community did not expect it either. She spent a happy year as Seeni's wife. No woman mocked or made fun of her. They looked at her with respect, as if she had attained some great new stature.

He did not find anything wrong with her. 'Hey, think well. The doctor has informed me that I will never be able to get babies. I don't have a uterus or something. If you start saying I never knew earlier, I will tell you to get out,' she had warned.

'I never think about that. Why are you getting all worked up?'

---

5 *Jimikkis*: Elaborate earrings worn by Indian women.

6 Mariamman: Another depiction of Goddess Shakti.

In truth, she had never been worked up about it. She felt it was a blessing to not have children. Singaram who lived in the far corner of the street was a massive drunk, but he was a hero in making his wife pregnant. He died suddenly one day. His wife Chandra was now a vegetable seller, dragging her kids with her in the vegetable cart. Ganga often felt like waking up the dead Singaram and spanking him.

Seeni's presence seemed like an armour. She went to work as usual. She dressed up for her own pleasure. She spent the money she had earned as she liked. She could spend or save. Seeni never interfered. Most important, the gossips in the neighborhood were silenced. Now, it seemed like they were all talking, like the floodgates had been opened.

She had become numb with shock when she knew the truth. Her heart still beats fast with shame remembering that moment. Seeni had not come home for two days. She was worried and scared when his phone went unanswered. She went in search of his distant office in Yelahanka[7] to enquire what had happened.

She was informed that he had died of a heart attack at work, a couple of days ago. She was stunned. 'Why didn't you inform me? I am his wife,' she had said, overwhelmed by anger and grief.

'Really? He has a wife and four children in Bommanahalli.[8] That is the official address in the company's register. We informed the family. They came and claimed

7 Yelahanka: A suburb of Bengaluru, towards the north of the city.

8 Bommanahalli: A locality in Bengaluru.

his body. You will know more if you go there. Do you want the address?'

She shook her head and left the place. The humiliation was unbearable. It was as if someone had dealt her an unexpected death blow. *Lopar*. Did you fool me so insidiously? A massive fire consumed the pit of her stomach. Shedding tears for him seemed like an insult to her self-respect.

She did not change her way of dressing after Seeni's death. She did not see any reason to. Her gossipy neighbours, though, expected her to transform into a sorrowful movie heroine. They relished in exhibiting a sorrow, which they felt she did not demonstrate.

Her mother had started searching for a partner already. 'How long will you be alone?' she nagged every day.

'I don't want another marriage. I prefer being single.'

'How will you be alone without a man?'

'Wait and see how I do it.'

'People will gossip.'

'Let them.'

Her mother was crazy. She had gossipmonger women in that area who pontificated to her. She mentioned a man's name to Ganga daily. That man disappeared before the sun set that evening.

This was how she had met that man this morning. A real fool. The one who told her that she should not keep Rajini's poster in her house. She had almost pushed him out.

Her mother was speaking incessantly. 'He is a widower with married children living in other towns.'

'Do you want me to marry an old man?'

Her mother was enraged. 'Well, do you expect a young, handsome man to come for you now? It is a big thing that he was willing to marry you, despite knowing everything about you.' Her mother started wailing. 'Who is there for you after I die? Who will help through good and bad? People around you will not let you live in peace.'

'That fellow had hundred conditions. What is his problem if I keep a picture of Rajini?'

Her mother beat her forehead. 'You stupid girl! You are like a kid, with no idea of life's priorities. That man who said that is different. The man I am now referring to is different. He has his own business and money it seems. You need not suffer doing housework. He will take care of you well. I will bring him over this evening. Wear a sari. Don't wear a churidar.'[9]

The Madiwala Lake was motionless. Everyone—her mother and the women who lived in her street—seemed to be strangling her. She could not understand what was the right thing to do. Mother kept insisting that she needed to find a partner. The neighbourhood seemed to indicate that it would accept her only if she lived with a man.

'He will take care of you. You need not go out and work as a maid.'

Some 'madams' she worked for did not have a job. They would be reading the newspaper or watching TV. They would cook a variety of dishes and wait for their husbands. Would

9 *Churidar*: Tight-fitting trousers worn by both men and women in the Indian subcontinent.

she have to wait that way too? What was interesting about that, she wondered. She would be dependent on her husband for every *paisa*.[10] That seemed like a massive humiliation to her. Oh well, let him arrive. I will set forth my conditions.

She rose. Her seething mind now felt more peaceful. Tiger danced with joy when she reached home. As if she had been missing for a while and was only now returning home. She wore a sari to placate her mother. Her mother came with a snack packet. That man came behind her, climbing the steps slowly. He had a smiling face, as if he were the most benign man in the world. He looked all right, she thought. He did not look old, but definitely looked as if he was her father. She had already told her mother that she would not prostrate before him and so her mother refrained from making that request. After the man had been welcomed with snacks and tea, she looked at him and said, 'I have to tell you about myself'.

Her mother looked at her in panic and gestured, asking her to remain silent.

'So, tell me,' he said with a smile.

'I will not stop working.'

'Who asked you to stop working?' A smile.

'I like wearing a comfortable churidar.'

'Ok wear it.' A smile.

'I have stuck Rajinikanth's poster in the terrace. You should not ask me to tear it down.'

'I won't ask that,' he laughed.

She felt confused. Why was he laughing?

---

10 *Paisa*: The smallest monetary unit in India, equal to one hundredth of a rupee.

'This dog will always be with me.'

'Let it be. A dog is good company.'

She kept quiet, unable to think of anything further to say. Her mother sported a triumphant look. The man with the smile was sitting with one leg upon the other, as if he already owned the house.

'I have a problem. I can't have children.'

'I know. I already have children. They won't bother you. They are married and live in other towns.'

She had not seen a man like this until now.

'When shall we organise the marriage?' asked her mother.

'Can I ask something?' he asked. 'This house has been leased, right?'

'Yes, why?'

'I want to know. I need to see the agreement papers.'

She was gripped with a strange sense of fear. Is he a policeman or an investigating officer? 'I don't understand what you are trying to convey.'

'There is no mortgage or loan on this house, right?

'No. Why are you asking?'

'Shouldn't I know all the details since I will soon become its owner?'

She felt a shooting anger.

'How will you become the owner?'

Her mother blinked. She made meaningless gestures at Ganga.

'In place of a dowry.'

'Stand up.'

'What?'

'Please get up. I bought this house with the money I earned with my own sweat and blood. How can a stranger like you make it your own?'

His face changed. The smile vanished. 'Then who the hell will marry you?' he snarled.

'I don't want marriage. Hey, go. Go away!'

'Kaliamma, I thought I was mistaken but your daughter is indeed an arrogant woman. I should not have come here believing your words.'

Her mother followed him down the steps, cursing Ganga.

Ganga got up and locked the door.

'From now on, this door will not be opened to any man,' she told Tiger. The snack packet her mother had bought was still there. *Thool pakoda.*[11] She lit the gas stove and made tea for herself. She switched on the television. Rajinikanth appeared before her.

Tiger lay with his head on her lap. The pakoda and tea tasted great.

'My way is a unique way,' declared Rajini. The women of the neighbourhood hid in shame.

'I need to buy a new *Kochadaiiyaan* poster tomorrow,' Ganga decided.

Original Tamil title: *Thanivazhi*

Translated by: Sukanya Venkataraman

11 *Thool pakoda*: A deep-fried snack made of chickpea flour, onions and spices.

# Punishment

Seshagiri Rao slurred in terror. Sweat ran down his face in rivulets. His drenched khaki shirt stuck to his back. The man standing in front of him seemed to grow infinitely, from earth to the heavens. Who was he? A messenger from the God of Death? Was that an arrow or spear in his hand? What kind of altercation was this? A single bullet was enough to kill him… Rao felt a chill in his stomach. The gun in his hand had vanished. He could not fathom how that had happened. It was in the fellow's hand now. Was this real or a Rajnikanth movie? He—a mere boy—was laughing, Rajni-style. There was even a whip in one hand now. Oh, that was only a shoulder bag used to carry books. He swung it around several times and hurled it. The bag shot across, swirling, morphing into a whip, and striking mercilessly on the back and the chest. 'Amma…' Seshagiri could only groan in Telugu '*Le, le, Pora, othu ra…oth…othu…*' (Hey, go away, no, no, don't don't …).

'*Nayina, nayina…!*' (Father, father!) Seshagiri woke with a start. His son Babu was standing before him.

'Why are you sleeping at this time *Nayina*? Aren't you going to work?'

Seshagiri wiped his eyes firmly and looked at his watch. It was 9.30 in the morning. 'I just dozed off. What is it?'

'I'm leaving for college. I don't have any money with me.'

'Did you have your breakfast?'

He got up without waiting for Babu's response, opened his purse, and gave his son a hundred-rupee note and some change. 'Spend it wisely,' he said as usual. Like his father. One of the lessons he had been taught—spend wisely.

'Don't sleep during the day. You won't even know if someone robs the house. The papers will go to town writing about the robbery in a policeman's house.' Babu looked at him and added with a smile, 'The whole city will read the paper before you read it' and hurried towards the front door.

Seshagiri laughed, 'Go on, you thief!'

He looked at Babu kick-starting his bike. 'Looks like you didn't read the paper today?' he heard Babu's faint voice as he closed the door. 'I remembered grandpa when I read it.'

'No, I haven't read it,' said Seshagiri to himself. The result of having slept fitfully the night before. The reason why he had dozed off after breakfast this morning. And that silly dream.

He went into the bathroom and washed his face with cold water. It seemed like he saw the boy's face—the one in his dream—in the mirror above the washbasin. He wiped his face quickly and came out into the hall. His father, *appa*, was smiling out of a garlanded, framed photo in his police uniform.

Seshagiri felt uneasy without reason whenever he saw that smile. He often thought of removing the photo and storing it somewhere. If he did that, though, he would have to answer Babu's questions. Babu had been his grandpa's favourite. Hadn't he said that today's paper reminded him of grandpa? What on earth was there in today's paper? Babu had taken after his grandpa, questioning, prodding …

'Hey, your mother died when you were a child. Everyone was amazed how I managed to bring you up despite my police duty. You wouldn't know, would you, how many times the superintendent screamed at me for being late? Or how often they posted me on duty in some remote area? All this has aged me before my time although I'm just 48 years old. I haven't married again for your sake! No harm in dozing away for a minute after breakfast.' Seshagiri chuckled, as he hurriedly got ready for work. He heard the jeep in the distance. In these 23 years, he had risen from being a sub-inspector to a Superintendent of police. A reward for his hard work. He felt satisfied when he gazed at his reflection in the mirror. He did have a slight paunch. Ah well, that added to a more authoritative persona.

He locked the house and left. A Central Minister was visiting from Delhi. Ah, that was a pain in the arse. Always posed logistical problems. Red alert. Threat of fundamentalists and terrorists…have to stop all other work and drive the others to ramp up security. Driving others came easily. The khaki dress could transform you the minute you wore it. The mere sight of it could terrorize the layman.

Why, even an innocent man would accept his guilt under its whip. And that was thrilling.

*'Seshu, remember. We can get to the truth by talking gently. Our khaki shirt is enough to make them shiver. We should never even go close to using the fourth-degree treatment.'*

Appa was an old-fashioned man. He would not know what cheats they are now. They are smart with ready answers. Not just that, they are tricksters. They spin stories like truth. Hell, they are able to even fool the lie detector. Nothing helped like a good spanking and caning—haven't we known that? Known since the days of our great, great grandfather.

*Appa walked alongside him.*

*'He confessed to his guilt after a good beating'.*

*'It is not right to intimidate an innocent man and lock him up, Seshu.'*

*'God, can you keep quiet? If the man isn't guilty, let them handle it in court and free him!'*

*'My boy, you say this even when you are aware of how the system works?'*

*'Shhhh...enough. Please keep quiet.'*

Seshagiri accepted the salutes of his constables and walked into his office confidently. The day's papers were unfolded on his desk. He bent down to look at the picture in the newspaper on top. Some prisoner had been freed after being declared innocent—after 23 years. Now he was middle aged. Emaciated, cheeks hollow, eyes like a *thevaangu* (slender loris) bewildered at the outside world. The photo captured him hugging his mother and weeping. Seshagiri had no inclination for such stories. The police did their duty. Who could do anything if the court did not investigate a case soon after?

Seshagiri scanned the story and understood why Babu had asked him if he had read the paper. He was furious as he read the story. These newspaper fellows knew about things even before he, a policeman, did. There were thousands of prisoners in jail, but if one man was being freed it became a big story. A nosy reporter had even visited the now freed prisoner's village and written a movie script. Seshagiri read the story again, line by line.

'I was not even 20 years old when they locked me up. I am now 43. I lost my entire youth. My sister was then 12 years old. Now she has a daughter who is 12. My cousin was two years younger than I was. She is now a grandmother. An entire generation has gone by in my absence. What you see now is a corpse. I died a long time ago. My whole family is destroyed spending, mortgaging all they owned trying to move the courts to free me.'

Ah, how good he was with his words! Seshagiri looked at the face intently. He was unable to identify it nor did he remember seeing it.This must be someone else. He swept it aside with a grunt, pressed the bell to summon a constable and asked him to remove the day's papers. He called his team and issued detailed commands on security preparations for the minister's arrival. The venue of the minister's speech needed to be inspected. He asked two sub-inspectors to accompany him.

There was some disturbance in the university. Students were raising flags against the central government. 'Do these boys come to study or protest?' mused Seshagiri. 'Thank God Babu does not involve himself in these useless protests. He has been a good student, wasn't he?'

His mind remained confused, disturbed for reasons he could not fathom even as he got into his jeep. He remembered the face he had seen in the day's paper. He tried to brush the image away but the eyes kept staring at him. Could there be any connection between today's dream and that story? The dream he had had in broad daylight? He was suddenly impatient. Felt the jeep was moving like a turtle.

'Hey, Raju, why are you going so slow? The minister will arrive and depart before we complete our inspection!'

'I am going at 60, Sir. That is the limit here,' was the smart alec's response.

'Sir is worried about his duty,' chimed in the others.

'We will reach soon, Sir. The venue is further away due to security concerns.'

Seshagiri straightened his back and looked around. Which road was this? He felt like he was on the shoreline drifting between a memory and a dream. Wasn't this the road that went to Gulbarga?

'We will reach Karnataka if we continue going on this road,' someone said.

He did not respond. Were they testing him on purpose? You could not trust anyone in this department.

'Have you come this way, Sir?'

'Perhaps long ago. What about it now? The minister is coming to Andhra, right?' That silenced them. He still felt unreasonably anxious. He must have woken up on the wrong side of the bed today. He attempted to calm himself down by closing his eyes.

The Andhra police jeep sped past his closed eyes. He seemed to stand nowhere. Was it a memory or a dream?

*'Have we entered Karnataka?' he was asking. 'We need to go to Gulbarga...' It was nine in the morning. School children in their uniforms were standing at the bus terminus, tittering like birds. 'This is Gulbarga...Don't stop here. Park the jeep closer to the main road.'*

*Why Gulbarga? Who cared? Information had been received. He needed to nab a fellow from here. Sukanya was in labour. His father volunteered to be at the hospital. 'You go, son,' he had said firmly. 'Your duty is most important. I am here for your wife. You go.'*

*His boss, the superintendent—had strict orders from Delhi to nab the culprit. Who was the criminal? Who knew? All he had was an unclear computer-generated drawing of the possible culprit's face.*

*'Wouldn't the Karnataka police know?' he had asked. He had been silenced. 'Shhhh... there is no need to tell their police anything. We need to show them we did what they couldn't do...'*

*'I don't care what you do. You need to nab a guy and bring him here.'*

*Seshagiri had a splitting headache. A crazy mob had demolished an old mosque somewhere. The retaliation had been sporadic bomb explosions on several trains all over. It was the police's duty to find out the criminal. The constable whom he had sent with the computer graphic picture the day before came back indicating a particular street. He had interrogated some people there and written down a name. The target was a college student. He would need to walk this way.*

*Seshagiri began losing his patience. He attempted to contact the hospital but could not reach them.*

*'There he comes, Sir.'*

*A young man with a bag on his shoulder was walking along. In his teens surely.*

*'Does he look like the computer-generated drawing?'*

*'Shut up!' ordered Seshagiri. He approached the youth gun in hand.*

*'Hey, Is it Fakruddin Ahmed?'*

*'Yes'.*

*'Ah, there you are .Get into the jeep.'*

*The boy opened his eyes wide, in fear. 'Why?' he asked in Kannada.*

*Seshagiri hit him on the head. 'Get in because I say so!' he shouted in Hindi. The boy started crying.*

*'Please let me go. I am going to college. I have exams next week. Please check with my Principal. I am a law-abiding student. Please…please…'*

*'Did you not think of all this when you planted bombs in trains?'*

*'Ayayo, which train? There is no connection between me and those incidents.'*

*He sobbed in little hiccups, lamenting in Hindi laced generously with Urdu. 'I know nothing. I am studying and have never done anything against the law. Ask anyone...' The boy shut up after the constable sitting next to him slapped him. He started whimpering. 'Ammi... Ammi...(Mother)'*

*Seshagiri received lavish praise from the superintendent when he deposited the boy at the police station in Hyderabad.*

*'He will confess with the thrashing he gets'.*

*He breathed in relief and rushed to the hospital. His father was sitting on a bench and appeared tired. He briefly nodded at his son.*

*'How is Sukanya?'*

*'She's fine but the baby was born dead.'*

*Seshagiri felt grief grip his stomach. He wanted to cry. His father stroked his back.*

*'Don't worry. She is young. There will be another child.'*

*He went to see Sukanya. She was sleeping. Father was right. She was young. There would be another baby.*

*'What happened to your mission?' his father asked when he came back.*

*'Done. We nabbed the fellow.'*

*'Do you know if it was the right one?'*

*He was furious. 'What the hell! You are always suspicious of my abilities. Have you ever praised me?'*

*Seeing the tears welling up in his eyes his father looked at him shocked.*

*'Why now dear, am I not proud of you?' he said gently. 'I was in the police force too. I asked because I fear that if it turns out to be the wrong man, he will lose his entire life.'*

*'Couldn't you have refrained from asking this question?'*

*His father did not respond.*

*That incident slipped from his mind as time went by. The case would go on and on in court. He would have retired by then. Days passed and he was more focused on escaping the admonishments of his boss, the superintendent.*

*The explosions continued... who was behind them? Catch him...catch him...it is him! How many arrests there had been!*

*'Do you know if it was the right man?' What kind of a question was that!*

*He felt a perverse pleasure in ordering the fellows 'into the police vans'. They got in like sheep, heads lowered and frightened. He felt his chest expand with a sense of power as he pushed the arrested behind bars.*

*His very being crowed in victory as they screamed 'Yes, I did it,' after a good beating.*

*'Was it the right man?'*

*Father continued asking him that question. He asked that question in front of Babu once. Seshagiri was outraged. 'I'm going to lock you up too, one day' he screamed. Babu refused to eat that day.*

*His father was alive until Babu was 10. He had lovingly brought up his grandson after Sukanya's death. Seshagiri cried bitterly when his father died, more out of guilt. But he also felt a sense of being liberated. His father would not question him any longer. Appa did not know that Seshagiri knew how to escape even if he did make mistakes. Consoling Babu had been the hardest part.*

He sat up with a start. Appa stood on the road blocking the jeep. Seshagiri stared at him unbelieving. Appa looked tired.

'Seshu!'

'Go, go away. Don't block the path!' Seshagiri muttered.

'Did you say something, Sir?'

'No, nothing,' he said, attempting to collect himself.

'We have reached the venue, Sir.'

Seshagiri felt weary, as if he had been on a long trip. His body ached. He stretched and got down from the jeep.

The university campus was a distance away. The central minister was afraid. The local minister was afraid. Why the hell were they afraid of these young boys? Round them all up; locking up for a few days without food and water will bring them to their senses. Simple.

Seshagiri swung into action. He needed to bring the sniffer dogs in tomorrow to survey the area. It was past midnight when he reached home.

Who was that sitting in the veranda on an easy chair? He was shocked. It was appa who was there, waiting like before. His face looked deeply distressed.

'Seshu!'

Was he crying?

Seshagiri felt like tearing his hair out. 'Who is that?' he roared.

'There is no one there, Sir,' said Raju, the driver.

'Oh, it seemed like someone was there,' muttered Seshagiri taking a deep breath as he unlocked the door and entered the house.

Babu usually went to bed at ten in the night. Seshagiri decided to look in on his son in the morning and went to sleep.

The call came from the police station at three in the morning. 'It appears that there is a group plotting to create trouble tomorrow in the University. There could be a conspiracy angle. They say the Minister's life could be at risk. A lot of pamphlets were found.'

Seshagiri felt a spurt of anger. How brazen could these fellows get to be? 'Who the hell are they? The Minister's security is paramount. I will come right away.'

He walked out of his house seething with anger. He decided not to wake up Babu and got into his jeep. His sub-inspectors updated him before he entered the university campus with a police team. There were notes written in red abusing the Minister. And many other slogans in red on the walls. Seshagiri could not even read properly through his rage. He thought there was also a Pakistani flag.

'What other evidence do we need? Let us round up the rascals, drag them all who are hiding, arrest them and lock them up as conspirators, traitors of the nation!'

'Yes Sir!'

The team acted briskly and dragged the students out like a herd of cattle from wherever they were. Those who protested were beaten with canes on their heads and backs. He looked on with satisfaction as they got into police vehicles like sheep.

A boy stopped before getting into a vehicle and looked back at him intensely. Seshagiri felt dizzy. Was it a dream or was this real? He felt an immense force charging forward to attack him. He was there, that *thevaangu*, with piercing eyes, part of that force, swinging his bag of books like a whip…

Seshagiri Rao's tongue slurred, his brows sweating.

He—Babu—laughed, rakishly, almost like Rajnikanth. He then vanished inside the vehicle as a constable smacked him on his head.

Original Tamil title: *Dandanai*
Translated by: Sukanya Venkataraman

# Murder

Old Somaiya Thaatha felt his eyes growing heavy. He would have drifted into a pleasant sleep if his stomach had not set up this continuous rumble. Though it was midday, the sun was mild. A margosa tree planted long ago with some forethought, had now grown tall with lush branches and spread out into a mountainous umbrella like the Govardhan hill held aloft by Krishna. It tempered the heat. Beneath its shade stood a permanent fixture, the string cot of Somaiya Thaatha. He would be found on this cot at all times, except when he was supervising the vegetable garden at the back of the house or had gone to the threshing yard. It created the impression of being a throne. As a matter of fact, he was the monarch here, and would remain one as long as the lands remained in his name; whatever he prescribed was law. This place was very convenient for him to sit. From here, he could keep an eye on everything that was going on in the household. The fear of old Thaatha made the women get on with their work without chatting. How can a house be run, if the women go on chattering?

Though he was reclining on the cot, Thaatha firmly resolved not to fall asleep and turned over on his side. The racket made by the children made one think that one had entered the marketplace. Yet, through all that din, Thaatha detected that the uniform whirr made by the grinding stones on which the women had been grinding millet, had stopped. He sat up with a jerk, shouting, 'Hey, what's all that noise for?' and looked at the platform in front. Gomathi and Nagalakshmi who were sitting on the ground facing each other across the quern, now started to grind again. He felt a sudden rush of anger. 'What's all that gossiping about, neglecting your work?'

Looking at each other with sidelong glances, the women lowered their heads and fell silent. Meenakshi who was grinding at the other quern, murmured to Saraswathi who sat opposite. 'The old thing has got eyes like torches.'

'Hey you kids there, no school today?'

'We are back from school, Thaatha.'

He noted that some of the children were in school uniforms. They were all 'Hey, you kid' for him. He did not remember any of their names. Nor could he tell whose children they were. This, in spite of the fact, that it was he who had christened every child.

'Thaatha, a baby has been born to Raju.'

'Which Raju?'

'Your elder brother's grandson. Please suggest a name for the baby.'

'Name it Natarajan.'

'But that's his eldest child's name. And it was you who named him.'

'I see. Call it Thyagarajan then.'

'That is the name of Chandran's son.'

'Which Chandran?'

'Oh well, leave it.'

After a lot of 'Not this' and 'Not that' a name would be chosen at last. He would completely forget the name in all this confusion. Still, the birth of a baby in the family always gladdened his heart. Whenever a baby was born to anyone in the family, it would at once be brought here to this margosa tree, wrapped up in a piece of cloth and placed in Thaatha's hands as he sat on his cot. Thaatha would look at it for a few seconds, enthralled by the vision of this freshly moulded earth. If it happened to be a boy, his joy would be doubled. He would then take out a rupee coin from the pouch tucked at his waist, place it in the child's tender young hand and bless him, 'May you grow up healthy and fortunate'. Even if a girl was born, Thaatha was not unduly grieved by it. The female population should be enough to match the number of males. That way, one needn't bring in girls from outside to marry into one's clan. A girl from outside spells danger. She would split the household, just as Thangappan's wife did. Thangappan set up a separate family all right, but did he achieve anything by it? We need children, lots of them. They are a family's strength. Like the large number of aerial roots that reach the earth and grow up into pillars that support the banyan tree. Thaatha had never allowed that hospital van with the red triangle anywhere near his house. One's land may be no bigger than one's palm, yet one would need men to get down into the field and work. That's why he exploded like an earthquake when Kumaresu ventured after much hesitation to mention it the other day.

'Thaatha, my wife and I are going to the hospital.'

'Why, what's wrong?'

'Nothing is wrong with our health. It's just that we want to consult the doctor.'

'What for?'

'We have got four children and that's enough. We don't want anymore.'

A sudden spurt of anger made the old man's moustache tremble.

'Hey, look, I am still very much alive. Have you started deciding all these things by yourselves? If you reduce the number of children you have, do you intend to invite outside labour to work in the fields?'

'We have produced enough children to meet the labour needs of our land.'

He looked towards the direction of that voice, taken aback. It must have been one of those women on the platform in front—one of those women who had not even lifted their heads and were engaged in grinding flour.

He asked Kumaresu, 'Which woman dared to say that?'

'Oh, let it go, Thaatha,' said Kumaresu trying to cover up. 'The government itself blares the message in street after street: "One is enough. None after two," it says.'

The old man roared: 'What else do you expect from a government run by a bunch of good-for-nothings? They just sit tight and don't respond to our applications for loan for digging a borewell or installing a pump. What else will they say except, "We are not going to help you and you know it quite well too. So why do you have children?" Forget about hospitals now. Go in and get on with your work.'

Kumaresu stood hanging his head. Someone from the platform in front seemed to say something.

'Who is that woman grumbling there?'

All of them were deeply engrossed in their work, their mouths sealed.

A tiny tot went on winding his string round a top, as he said, 'They are asking, "Are we just childbearing machines?"'

As Kumaresu lunged at him, his hand raised to strike, the boy ran away, laughing.

The old man trembled from head to foot. 'The cheek she has! Who said that?'

Nagalakshmi who was grinding millet got up in a flash. While everyone watched her in panic, she sprang down from the platform and looked up at the old man, straight in the eyes.

'It was I who said it,' she said flushing, her lips trembling slightly. Four hours of grinding flour sitting on the floor had crumpled up her sari and its border was now well above her ankles. The part of it that covered her breast had a hole in it. Covered in flour up to her elbows, her face and head, she stood enveloped in a white haze that gave her an eerie appearance.

Amazed and embarrassed, Thaatha looked at her thin, nearly fleshless, frame and fierce face. Though she was his grand-daughter—his daughter's daughter—she had never spoken to him face to face. But the degree and manner of her relationship did not merit any attention now.

'Are we to go on bearing children like sheep and cows? Don't we need some rest?'

Finding the whole lot of them standing absolutely silent around him, the old man felt peeved. 'These females seem to be getting so insolent nowadays. Do you get so much free time here that you spend it in idle chatter? If you got any more leisure, you'd begin to get out of the house and watch films. God created woman for the sake of procreation—to increase our progeny. And listen, you faceless menfolk, you better make this point clear to your wives. Away now! Go and do your work, all of you!'

Ignoring the presence of the gasping woman standing in front of him, Thaatha picked up his towel from the bed, shook it and threw it over his naked chest, struck the floor with his stick and called out. 'Hey, you fellows, somebody come with me to the threshing yard,' and moved out. As all of them dispersed and went away to attend to their work, Nagalakshmi came and sat before her quern, her face tense with humiliation, as if she had suffered a defeat.

'Do you know how I feel at times? I feel like twisting the old geezer's neck.' The grinding women were not taken aback. They just smiled knowingly, as if it was some joke. Only young Chellam who was rocking her baby sister in a cloth cradle was startled, because of the rage that she saw on Nagalakshmi's face.

'Well, if that cannot be done, all that can be done is to end one's own life,' said Nagalakshmi. Even this remark was greeted with silence by the other women. It looked as though they were reluctant to say anything.

Those words made Chellam freeze with fear. What had come over aunt Nagalakshmi today? She had been down with fever sometime back and had been cross with everyone ever since. When the fever raged very high, Nagalakshmi had once shaken off her woollen blanket and had started to run screaming, 'Chellathayi is calling me!' Chellam's father and two of his sisters had dragged her back and made her lie down. Then, with tears in their eyes they had burnt camphor and performed a puja and appealed to Thaatha.

'This must be the work of some evil spirit,' he said. 'Go hang a bunch of margosa leaves at the door.' They had broken off a whole branch of the margosa and placed it inside. A bunch of margosa leaves was also hung above the locked door of the room where Chellathayi had hanged herself.

As for the reason why Chellathayi had hanged herself, little Chellam had no idea.

It had happened some 12 years ago when Chellam had been but a baby of a few months old. Chellam's name was also Chellathayi. It had become Chellam after the elder Chellathayi hanged herself. Her aunts used to tell her that Chellathayi's ghost made its appearance now and then. In the blackest new moon nights, the ghost could be heard weeping, perched on the margosa tree. However, it never seemed to have harmed Thaatha in any way, though he was always seated on the cot beneath the tree as if a nail kept him firmly in place. Even the ghost would be scared of Thaatha, thought Chellam. Moreover, this was a female ghost. Was it likely that a dead woman would muster the sort of courage that she never had while alive? No.

As he looked at the children at play in their school uniforms, Somaiya Thaatha remembered something. It was time for lunch, wasn't it?

'Hey, did you all have your lunch?'

'No Thaatha. The rice has not been cooked yet.'

'Atrocious! It must be half past one now. Isn't the meal ready yet? Whatever have these women been doing?'

Picking up the stick he had left at the edge of his bed and planting it firmly on the ground, he stood up. His stomach stretched itself up as well and began to rumble. 'Why isn't cooking done yet?' he roared.

The whole courtyard shrank in silence at that roar. In the recent past, he had become accustomed to such silences. His reaction to it had been a frustrated anger every time,

and it was the same again this time.

As he walked towards the kitchen mumbling, 'Nothing seems to be under control in this house any longer,' he was assailed by another worry: What will things be like when my eyes are closed for ever?

Raju's wife Rasamma was sitting outside the kitchen, mashing boiled greens and lentil. Sitting in the heat of the firewood stove, had given her face a dark flush.

'Is it your turn to cook today? Why is the meal not ready yet?'

Not bothering to turn her head even slightly towards Thaatha and without any pause in her mashing, Rasamma answered: 'It's not my turn today. It's actually Kamala akka's turn. She has been taken ill and so they fetched me from the field. I had to boil the lentil after coming from there and then cook rice for the whole battalion here. Surely, it will take some time, won't it?'

Ignoring the discontent and weariness in her voice, the old man asked, 'Which Kamala do you mean? Kumaresu's wife?'

'Yes.'

'What is the matter?'

'The usual thing. Dizziness and vomiting.'

'Pregnancy?'

She nodded assent, without looking up.

'So that's all,' said the old man, quite relieved. 'You could have asked someone to help you, if it was getting late, couldn't you?'

'Each woman has some work or the other.'

'Look at that girl Chellam standing there, she is just rocking the cradle. Why don't you call her?'

'Why make her do this sort of work at such a tender age?'

'Doing such chores when necessary can't harm her. After all, she's only a girl child. And quite old enough, I should say.'

'She's only 12, Thaatha.'

'Only 12? My wife was only eight when I married her. Even then she knew how to cook *kulambu* (a tamarind-based side dish) and rice. Well, how long will it be for lunch now?"

'Almost ready. You can go now.'

As soon as he returned to the courtyard, he called out loudly, 'Chellam, Chellam!'

As the girl ran up to him swiftly like a sparrow and stood before him, he looked absentmindedly at her. She had brought the end of her half-sari round her waist and tucked it in like a grown up. Her young breasts were budding points behind that sari.

'What's that in your hand?' he asked.

'A book.' She opened it and showed him.

'How did you get it?'

'It is younger brother's. A text book.'

'What do you want it for, you girl?'

'Oh, I am just looking at it. It's nice. With lovely pictures. I feel like reading it.'

'Leave it. Don't waste your time on such useless things. Do what is proper for a girl to do. Go in and help Rasamma in the kitchen. Lay out the plates and pour out water for drinking and all that. Go on.'

As Chellam returned to the platform, her head hanging down, Nagalakshmi gave her a mocking smile. Chellam felt that she had somehow been insulted. She felt a stab of sorrow and a film of tears covered her eyes.

This Thaatha's neck had to be twisted, certainly, just like Aunty says. As she wended her way towards the kitchen after thrusting the book back into her brother's bag, her path was barred by a hen that kept pushing her beak stylishly forward and backward, leading a procession of chicks.

Chellam drove it away angrily. 'Shoo! Shoo! You wretch!'

The whole brood scattered clucking wildly.

The meal was at last over. All the uncles—maternal and paternal—who had gone to work in the fields had returned and had their lunch. Their wives, who had gone to the gardens had also returned, bathed and eaten. When the *athai*s (the sisters of these men) took their food and came back, the millet querns that had enjoyed a brief rest began to grind again.

A post-prandial heaviness hung over the household. The aunts seemed to be turning their grinding stones in a half-sleep. A low snore emanated from Thaatha who now lay stretched on the cot beneath the margosa. There was no sign of the children anywhere. The baby was asleep in its cloth cradle.

Chellam went past the kitchen, opened the small bamboo gate of the backyard and entered the kitchen garden. As she skipped along, holding up the hem of her half-sari, past the beds of egg plants, okra and tomatoes, butterflies fluttered by her side. She raised her arm to catch them and 'plop' went her feet, into the wet bed, muddying her skirt all round its edge.

'See, you butterflies? See what's happened, all because of you!'

Beyond the vegetable garden lay the fields. Sparrows were perched on the ripe corncobs. She drove them away, in the manner of Thaatha: 'What? We go to work and you go to steal? Off! Off with you!'

Swiftly the sparrows rose in the air. As Chellam raised her head to watch, the birds were gone, in the twinkling of an eye, beyond the wall that stood at the edge of the field.

'If only I had wings,' thought Chellam, 'I could go there and come back, without anyone noticing my absence. I needn't then bother about this Thaatha at all.'

In the center of the lush green fields stood a pump on raised ground. She climbed the slope with quick steps as if it were a slide. Upon reaching the top, the school on the other side of the wall became visible. A girl's school. Girls of her age in long, yellow skirts and white half-saris wearing their hair in two plaits tied with yellow ribbons. Girls who carried books in their hands, and inspired a sense of awe in her.

'That's a school run by Christians,' her father had told her.

'What does "Christian" mean?"

'They are a different people. They worship a different God.'

'But please let me go there. It's so close by.'

'No, my girl. Thaatha would never allow it.'

'Why not?'

'He says that they follow an entirely different scripture and we should not read all that.'

Then let me go to the school where little brother studies.'

'Thaatha would say "No!"'

'You plead with Thaatha, please.'

The roar of Thaatha's anger that day reduced the sheep and the cows and the hens and the sparrows to a stunned silence. The leaves of the margosa stood motionless.

'There's no need for a woman to be educated at all is there? Grinding millet and cooking don't call for any educational qualification.'

'Well, the girl seems to be rather keen on it. I think we can let her study at least till she reaches puberty?'

'No. We can't allow such things. As it is, women have started to speak impudently. If they also get educated, they wouldn't stay under our control. The honour of the house

would be sullied.'

The school playground was visible as Chellam looked from the top of the mound. There was a basket-like thing fixed at a high point into which girls kept throwing a ball that was too big for their hands. Girls who were older than Chellam. Those girls would not have had any Thaatha in their homes, thought Chellam. In this house, no girl older than Chellam could step out of the gate. Married women do not go out anywhere except to work in the gardens. Unmarried girls could only go round and round the courtyard, if at all they got any respite from work. Chellam used to go along with other children to the car festival and other such occasions in the temple. Even that had been stopped for the past two years.

'You needn't go for all that," Thaatha had said. "Why go year after year? And pester us to buy this and that? This place is not littered with money, you see.'

This place is a fort. It had a huge door—just like a fort—a door made of a zinc sheet and painted in rust colour. Beyond that door, lay the wide world. A world of laughter and colour and music. Where women walked about boldly, without any male escort. Where they opened their handbags, took out money and bought things. Where they wore chic undergarments beneath their saris and blouses, just like the heroines in films.

Chellam used to describe such things to her aunts when she returned from the fairs. It was she who had told Nagalakshmi that a box with a small screen was available in the shops. Films are shown on these screens and her father had said that people buy and keep the boxes in their homes these days.

'That thing is called a TV,' her eldest uncle's son Ramu had explained, adding, 'You can watch films on it while sitting at home.'

'What? Sitting at home?' Aunt Saraswathi and aunt Gomathi stopped grinding and opened their eyes wide. Aunt Nagalakshmi tut-tutted without pausing in her grinding. 'Oh, forget all that. Just get on with your work all of you.'

'But Ramu, do you know how much this thing costs?'

'Well above a thousand and five hundred.'

'Oh, my! That much, eh?'

'I told you to get on with your work, didn't I?'

'But akka, we work ever so hard cooped up indoors the whole day. Have we ever asked to be taken to the cinema?

No. If they bought one of these things, we can sit and watch it in the evening, can't we?'

'What a stupid girl you are! Can anyone spend even a paisa without the permission of that geezer under the margosa tree?'

Saraswathi and Gomathi hung their heads and started to grind again.

'I feel like running away.'

'Where will you go?'

Silence greeted the question as if to say that there was no answer to it.

'It's enough if we get a TV. There is no need to run away.'

Then let each one of us tell this to her husband. If the men folk gang up together and ask the old man, the thing can be done.'

But no, the thing was not done. The fact is, the matter never went as far as old Thaatha. The men folk themselves were not agreeable to the suggestion. They said, money could be spent only for things of utility. If the women sit back watching TV they won't pay enough attention to work. Chellam's father's mother and the other grandmothers added their mite, saying, 'Look at these women hankering after this and that! What makes them brash enough to ask?'

The girls in yellow skirts and white half-saris bobbed up and threw the ball and burst into peals of laughter. Chellam wouldn't mind not having a TV, if only she could go to that school! But for this Thaatha, her father would have given her permission.

Thaatha made a general sort of proclamation one day: 'Money and women should both be kept under lock and key. Otherwise both would give you the slip.'

Chellam now said aloud: 'When will Thaatha die?'

Sparrows flew above the corncobs.

'Will he never die?'

'Never. Never,' the sparrows seemed to screech. It seemed that unless someone twisted his neck just like aunt Nagalakshmi had said, he wouldn't die. Otherwise one must end one's own life like that Chellathayi. But Chellathayi! Why did you hang yourself?

The bell rang in the school. The girls poured out, all white and yellow, like butterflies. Chellam lifted her hands up as if she was flying. She became one with that crowd, in a confluence of her self with theirs.

'Hey, Chellam! Your baby sister has woken up and is crying. Come here. Your mother has gone to the field.'

'Let it cry,' said Chellam without moving.

Somaiya Thaatha was hovering between sleep and wakefulness. It was a breezeless, stuffy night. It was two days, he remembered, past the new moon day and pitch dark. Directly above his head was a circle of mosquitoes buzzing as they wheeled round. He pulled at the sheet that came up to his neck so as to cover his face. Even with his eyes shut, his ears were attuned to the tiniest sounds and were awake and alert: The crying of babies in the nook of the innermost parts of the house. The jingle of bangles. The bark of the street dogs. Even the breathing of the cows in their shed could be heard distinctly on some nights. During sleepless nights, Thaatha would take up his stick and go for long walks. The smell of manured soil, the cows and sheep in the shed, the crying of babies—these vitalized his mind. Tonight he slept fitfully; if he got up, sleep might desert him completely.

A sound of someone crying. Thaatha was immediately alert. Removing the sheet from his face, he looked around. He was not able to guess where the sound came from. Was it from inside the house? Or from the margosa tree?

A sudden sweat drenched his whole body. It sounded like a woman weeping. The tree stood still above him. It could also be the wail of a dog—a thin, helpless moan as if it had been beaten. Perhaps it had seen a bad dream. There is no rule that says that a dog can't dream, is there?

Thaatha turned on his side. His eyes were open. The house stood like a shadow—the shadow of a black monster. This monster was easier to handle during daytime. Now in the dark, it appeared fearsome and beyond his grasp. Secrets are born from this darkness—secrets that have escaped his notice. And they haunt the place like ghosts. Women folk happen to be the first targets of these ghosts.

'"Are we to go on bearing children like sheep and cows?" Well, was that the way for a female to talk?' thought Thaatha, with rising anger. 'No, this was certainly some ghost talking. Even that slip of a girl—Chellam—had started asking strange questions. By the way, was her name Chellam or Chellathayi?' A shiver ran through his body as if in response to a sudden gust of wind. It was in that locked room, which now stood as a silhouette in the darkness before his eyes that the 14-year-old girl Chellathayi had hanged herself. Foolish girl. Why did she hang herself? Her father use to boast that she was a clever girl and would have become a graduate, if only she had been born a boy. She used to flit about like a chirpy bird through the fields and woods. But it is not proper for a girl to venture beyond the front door, once she has reached puberty. That's what I had told her. And that was what roused her anger. But was that any reason for anyone to die? And now she comes weeping.

There seemed to be a stir of leaves. Thaatha sat up with a start. Some dark shadow seemed to walk by. Again he broke out into a sweat. A slight panic gripped his belly.

'Who's that?' he asked, his tongue producing an indistinct slur.

The shadow hurried along.

'Go away, Chellathayi, I'll make an offering for you, please go away.' His legs went limp and his whole body was drenched with sweat.

When he woke up in the morning, the sun fell hot on his face. It was when he returned in the noon sun after going round the fields that Saraswathi ran up to him gasping.

'Kamalakka is not well. She has to be taken to the town hospital.'

'Why, what is the matter?'

'She is losing blood. A high temperature. Delirium.'

'I thought she was pregnant.'

'She was. But she aborted.'

'When?'

'Last night.'

The memory of things he had seen in the night made Thaatha shiver again.

'Must be the attack of some spirit.'

'No, Thaatha. She must be taken to the hospital immediately.'

'You heard what I said. Go, hang a bunch of margosa leaves on the threshold. We will make an offering to Chellathayi today.'

Saraswathi began to cry.

'Why, woman, what are you crying for?'

'It is not a case of any spirit or ghost. Akka has to be taken to the hospital. The menfolk have all gone to the fields. There is no male member at home now. The children have all gone to school.'

'What do you want me to do?' said Thaatha in a huff. 'You women must wait till the men return. Give her some water boiled with dried ginger. How can anyone get sick all of a sudden like that?'

Saraswathi stuffed the free end of her sari into her mouth and sobbed.

Chellam, who was rocking her baby sister in the cradle, noted that the faces of her aunts were woebegone. There was some secret they shared, talking in whispers. Hearing some noise in the front corridor, Chellam ran there and looked. Uncle Raju had returned from the fields. She came back running and told her aunts.

'Uncle Raju is back.'

Nagalakshmi and Saraswathi dashed at once to the front corridor, not even waiting to dust off the flour from their saris, and they failed to notice that Chellam accompanied them.

'Kamalakka must be taken to the hospital at once,' they said.

'What's the matter?'

Fear had dried up Aunt Nagalakshmi's tongue. 'It seems she had asked the midwife to come last night to have an abortion. The midwife has messed it up.' Aunt Saraswathi began to cry. Shock was evident on Uncle Raju's face.

'So you women have started doing all these things, have you?'

'Please, please don't ask anything now. Just take her along. Thaatha needn't be told the details.'

By the time Uncle Raju got some money from Thaatha and came back with a taxi, the evening shadows had set in. The roof was shaking with Kamalakka's screams. The hens and chickens lay huddled and silent. The sheep and the cows refused to yield milk in their agitation.

Thaatha kept repeating, 'We will make an offering to Chellathayi.' The women in the family—the maternal and paternal aunts—were crying as if death had already occurred. Perhaps that was the reason why they were not able to cry when Kamalakka's dead body returned in the middle of the night from the hospital. On the contrary Aunt Nagalakshmi's eyes reflected an intense hatred and anger.

Uncle Kumaresu alone cried, beating himself on his head again and again. 'Oh, I am the one to blame, I am a sinner.'

The children were shocked and bewildered and when their sleepy eyes wouldn't stay awake anymore, lay down and curled up and went to sleep wherever they liked. Chellam did not feel sleepy. The things spoken by her aunts and their weeping were beyond her grasp. Her stomach felt churned up looking at the sight of Kamalakka who was hale and healthy last morning but now lay as a white-faced corpse. All the figures seated in the courtyard dimly lit by the shallow open wick lamp, were like small ghosts, while Thaatha—who occupied the central position prominently—looked like a big ghost. Chellathayi must have hanged herself, suffocated by being in the midst of this crowd. And Kamalakka must have died for the same reason.

Somaiya Thaatha's eyes were heavy with sleep. Those who were sitting in the courtyard had all gone into the house to sleep. Kumaresu's lamentations were heard intermittently. Later, even that died down. This kind of death had never occurred in this house before, thought Thaatha. There had never been even a miscarriage at any time. This was certainly the work of some evil spirit. That's why he had felt a sudden chill of fear the night before, when he saw something moving like a shadow. That's why his tongue had uttered the name of Chellathayi. He ought to have arranged for that offering of food for her ghost much earlier. It was wrong on his part to have been negligent.

The thought of Thangappan somehow intruded into his consciousness now. A hefty, well-built young man, he was. No suitable girl was found in the clan for him and they had to get a wife from Madurai. The girl had some education and used to question everything. She seemed to have worked on him and when, one fine day, Thangappan had stood firm like a pole before him and said, 'We are moving out to set up house separately.' Thaatha got the shock of his life.

'How dare you say such a thing?' Thaatha had shouted. While the whole lot of them stood silent, Thangappan stood defiantly, while his wife said, 'This is a prison, a haunted house. Our only hope of respite lies in escaping from this house.' Thaatha now remembered how Thangappan had followed her out of the door.

Thaatha had not found it possible to forgive Thangappan and his wife even today. Nor did he feel curious to know how he had fared—well or ill. But then, has any man who listened to his woman ever prospered? He thought of his wife Sornam. She was as silent as the cow in the shed. She hadn't ever contradicted him—not even a single day. The truth was that he didn't remember if she ever spoke at all. She had borne him ten children, feeling duty bound to do so.

Though Thaatha's ears could now hear clearly the soft jingle of bangles, the rustle of cloth and the chill wind, his eyes felt too weary to open. He felt something at his neck. There was something heavy crushing him. His body trembled. A dream? Or was it real? He gasped with fear.

'Chellathayi! Please leave me. I will make an offering for you,' he cried, but felt that the words were smothered by someone. He tried to open his eyes and shout but failed in his attempt.

When Chellam awoke in the morning, Thaatha was laid out on the funeral bier alongside Kamalakka. He lay swaddled in a white cloth, with his face alone visible. People from the neighbourhood were seated at the *pyol*.[1]

The aunts were all hanging their heads, not even talking amongst themselves.

Chellam's grandmother—her father's mother—was telling someone and crying, 'He kept moaning that he would make an offering.'

The huge zinc door at the entrance to the house now stood wide open.

Original Tamil title: *Kolai*
Translated by: Gomathi Narayan
First published in *The Guilty and Other Stories* (New Delhi: Indialog Publications, 2002)

1 *Pyol*: A raised platform along the outer veranda of a house.

# Poison

She felt as if she had drowned in the inky darkness that surrounded her. The mango and jackfruit trees that had spread their branches over the entire backyard served to blacken the darkness further. Today, even the stars had stopped blinking their eyes and had gone into mourning. Rangamani shivered slightly. She felt that the blood that coursed through her body had bonded with the five elements. She had the illusion that some sign from her had turned the sky dark, shrunk the wind into itself, and dried up all water.

'Rangamani, Rangamani.' She sat immobile as a stone, staring at the darkness. 'Why are they fussing and panicking like this?' she thought, extremely annoyed.

'Rangamani, Rangamani,' coming through the darkness, the furtive voice sounded terrifyingly discordant. She drew up her knees and buried her face between her legs. But still the heart-rending cry could be heard, quite clearly: 'O *aatha*! O mother who bore me! I can't bear this. O no, I can't.'

Rangamani's arms, which held her legs, now stiffened. The muscles on her face went taut and her eyes burned as if they had caught fire. A loud moan was heard—*huhum*,

*huhum*, which sounded like a smothered scream. They would have gagged the woman with bunched up rags. Screams were not supposed to reach the menfolk, who were sleeping in the front quarters of the house. That was the way Pechiamma's daughter-in-law Minakshi had met her death—by suffocation.

What a shame! She was dead and gone before she could even hear her mother's shout: 'O it's a boy!' Minakshi had been quite weak even before. She had given birth to girl after girl six times in a row and had lost every one of them. The trauma that all this had caused her must have been severe indeed. Rangamani had a clear recollection of her meeting with Minakshi a week before her delivery. Thinking over it now, she felt even on that day Minakshi had been quite dead. Her face had been pale like that of a cadaver. Her eyes were sunken pits, distraught with fright. As soon as they fell upon Rangamani, they turned panic stricken.

'O no! What brought you here, Rangamani? Go away, go away,' she had cried, pressing herself against the wall like a gecko.

That was the day when Rangamani first hated herself. 'Alright, I'll go,' she had said and got up. Minakshi had suddenly lunged towards her and taken hold of her wrist.

'Listen. This time, if I give birth to a girl again, I won't survive.'

Minakshi's grip had been a fierce one. Like that of the monitor lizard. Like that of a corpse. Those words made Rangamani feel threatened. There was some kind of challenge in them. As though she was to blame for Minakshi giving birth to a series of female offspring. It now occurred to her that she had sat in Pechiamma's back veranda that day just as she was sitting here today. The memory stirred her feeling of guilt afresh.

Rangamani sat up straight. Her old habit made her ears prick up to listen. Nothing could be heard.

Oh you wretched women, have you suffocated her? All of a sudden, a child's cry was heard. A healthy, loud scream. Boy or girl? One couldn't tell from the voice. But one could tell from what accompanied it. If it happened to be a boy, the whole universe would wake up to rejoice. Here, the universe was that which was contained within the front quarters of the house. A mere flicker of the eyes from the front quarters can activate the rest of the house or doom it to limp listlessness. It was the bounden duty of the rear quarters to keep the front quarters contented. Any dereliction in this respect would result in a loss of status for the beings of the rear quarters.

Thoo! You bunch of helpless corpses! You shameless, prideless women! You have humbled and demeaned yourself just for the sake of the food and shelter that he gives you, you perpetrators of the deadliest sins!

A weak moan was heard. Then came wave upon wave of loud sobs. So the mother had not died of suffocation; she is crying. Crying as if she has suffered a great loss. The helpless woman.

'Rangamani, Rangamani,' the voice was edgy with urgency. 'Come on, Rangamani.'

Her petrified body now straightened itself. Her face was distorted and ugly. As she walked in the direction of the voice, she felt as if she had left her body behind and entered another one.

Under the rays of a small kerosene lamp, lay Gomathy on a bed, her hair reaching down to the floor like a black cobra.

In the dense silence that held the room in its grip, Gomathy's sobs were loud and clear. The shadows cast on the walls by those present in the room appeared monstrous. Rangamani walked very slowly, as if she was dragging the weight of all their corporal bodies along with her. At Gomathy's side lay a bonny baby—ah, a girl.

Curious, how all these girls looked so bonny. The baby gave her a dazed unfocused look. She felt her belly going limp. From deep within her, gushed out a flood of love: O my little darling! Gomathy who had been sobbing with her eyes shut, now gave a start and opened her eyes. At the sight of Rangamani, she took fright and said, 'Oh no! No! Go away, go away!'

Gomathy's mother covered her mouth with her hand. 'Shut up. Think of what your husband said before sending you here,' she said in a throaty whisper. 'He said he wouldn't admit you into the household if you came back with a girl child. Didn't he?'

Gomathy turned her face away, covered her mouth and cried. Rangamani bent down. The baby suddenly started to suck its finger furiously. The slurp-slurp of its sucking gave

Rangamani a slight panic. She took out the grains of paddy that she kept tucked at her waist and inserted them expertly into the baby's nostrils.

The baby gasped a couple of times. The sucked finger came loose and slipped down. The shadows around her were released from their daze and moved out. Rangamani wrapped the still warm baby in an old rag and tucking it under her arm, went out noiselessly to the backyard.

'Are you male or female?' Without giving her an answer, it kept moving round and round and kicked her jauntily. 'You kick well, you must be a male.' It shook itself again and again and bobbed up. Then it leapt and rolled around with a tinkle-tinkle. 'What? Are you wearing an anklet? You mean to tell me that you are a female, do you?'

Shanbagam stroked her belly slowly. This—here is a leg. And this—an arm. Gluck. Gluck. The leg and the arm moved away. She felt like laughing. What? You naughty thing! Giving my hand the slip even now, are you? The more she thought about it, the more amazing it seemed. It seemed a momentous matter to carry another life inside oneself. Then came the awesome thought: this responsibility has been entrusted to me because I am considered trustworthy. I will take good care of you. Have no fear. She felt inexplicably moved.

Shanbagam looked round her. Mother Earth herself seemed to be pregnant. The shadow of the mango tree stretched as far as the well in the backyard. The tree was in full bloom and its fragrance greeted her the moment she set her foot into the yard. Under the tree was a cement bench. A bench that had seen three generations. A bench built for Kumaresu's father's grandmother by her doting husband, when she was pregnant. It was Kamakshiakka who had given her this information soon after Shanbagam came to this house as a new bride, putting her right foot first on the threshold.

'There seems to be a Taj Mahal in your house,' she had teased Kumaresu and laughed. The recollection of how he had stared at her, completely nonplussed, made her laugh even now. The great-grandfather had been wiser than the one who had built the Taj Mahal. For he had built the bench while the woman was still alive. Like Mumtaj, this great-grandmother too seems to have borne fourteen children and then died in childbirth. But the only children who had survived were Kumaresu's grandfather and his younger brother.

As she placed the aluminium pot on the washing stone by the well in the backyard and began to sift the stones and wash the rice in water, she thought of Kamakshiakka. Kamakshi was full term pregnant now. Shanbagam had never seen her lying on this bench. She always lay curled up in the dark veranda by the kitchen. When Shanbagam asked her, 'Akka, why don't you lie down on the bench and get some fresh air?' she had replied, 'You need to have certain qualifications for all that, my dear.' This would be her eighth delivery. All the seven babies born to her had died. All had been girls.

Shanbagam found it incomprehensible why Kamakshi should flinch even from looking at light, as though she was labouring under some burden of shame. Her husband hardly seemed to speak amiably to her. It was surprising that she became pregnant at all.

'Akka, why don't you consult a doctor?'

'But there's nothing wrong with me, is there? I am quite alright.'

'No, akka. If every child born to you has died, there must be some reason. Maybe there's something wrong with your blood.'

'There's nothing wrong with me,' said Kamakshi. 'Let's just say that this is my fate— what Brahma has written on my head. Just as Devaki went on bearing child after child, in our mythology.'

Shanbagam felt confused. 'Won't you go to the hospital for your delivery?' she asked.

'It has always been at home.'

'Oh God! Don't do that akka. The town hospital is quite a good one. The lady doctor there is very capable. She'll take good care of you. Your baby is going to be alright this time. Just wait and see.'

Kamakshi suddenly looked up at her. A flash lit up her anaemic eyes like lightning and died as quickly as it had appeared. Kamakshi bent her head and said, 'Let's see.'

'I will have it only in the hospital,' said Shanbagam.

'Yes, go there,' said Kamakshi wearily. 'You are an educated woman. Besides you are from another village. Kumaresu is sure to listen to what you say.'

'But you'd better ask him whether he would say, "It's alright", even if you happened to have only a girl,' laughed Janaki, Kumaresu's second elder brother's wife, who was grinding flour.

'She must have said that jokingly,' thought Shanbagam.

'Is it in our hands, whether we give birth to a girl or a boy,' she asked.

The others hung down their heads in silence.

Janaki said softly, 'Why don't you ask Kumaresu?'

It was quite late by the time Kumaresu returned from the shop that night. And he was in quite a temper even as he entered. 'Let me not ask him any questions today,' thought Shanbagam and postponed it.

Now she remembered that she had completely forgotten to ask him. The women in this household were all natives of this village, all of them being intermarried according to the custom of marriage between certain first cousins. When Kumaresu's turn for marriage came, there was no girl available among relations. Finding no girl within the village either, they had chosen Shanbagam from another village. Kumaresu was modern, educated. If she asked him whether he wanted a boy or a girl, he was likely to laugh and say, 'What a foolish question!'

'Shanbagam! The water for the rice is on the boil. How long do you take for washing the rice!'

'Coming Janakiakka.' Quickly sifting and draining the rest of the rice, she took it inside. In the veranda, Kamakshi was lying down on her side, eyes closed. Her large pregnant belly lay on the ground semi-detached from the emaciated body. Janaki was working at the grinding stone. As Shanbagam poured the rice into the boiling water in the rice pot, she thought she heard someone knocking at the junk room at the back of the house. Janaki, who had just got up after washing the grinding stone, said, 'Let me go and look' and went back. When Shanbagam came out, she found Supputhayi who lived in the last house on the street sitting there. Upon seeing Shanbagam, she smiled briefly.

'When is this one due?' she asked.

'Plenty of time left—two months,' said Janaki. 'By the way, that Gomathy in the house opposite yours—she may have it anytime now, it seems.'

'She has delivered. Last night, it was,' said Supputhayi.

While the rest of them just sat still with an air of expectancy, Shanbagam asked eagerly, 'Boy or girl?'

'It died,' said Supputhayi, looking at the others.

'O God! Why?' said Shanbagam.

Supputhayi got up as if she had not heard the question at all. Looking at Kamakshi who had turned pale at hearing the news that she had just given, she let out a brief sigh. 'May God open His eyes and bless you at least this time.'

Kamakshi suddenly started to sob. Greatly distressed at this, Shanbagam held her shoulder and consoled her,

"Don't cry akka, don't cry. Let's go to the hospital this time. Everything will turn out alright."

'What's that about the hospital?' asked Supputhayi.

'Shanbagam says we must go to the hospital.'

Supputhayi looked her up and down and shook her head. 'It seems a new woman has come to our place recently—someone called a "health worker". I wondered if that woman had turned up here. She seems to blabber on about some cradles and what not.'

'What's that?' asked Kamakshi.

Supputhayi raised her voice in rebuke: 'That sort of thing is not for us. What about our prestige? You just keep quiet, will you?' Looking at Janaki, she whispered, 'In any case, our Rangamani is always there, isn't she?' Then she left.

'Who is this Rangamani, akka?' Shanbagam asked.

'She comes to help during childbirth. An unmarried, single woman.'

'Why didn't she marry?'

'She's just a wretched orphan. What man will marry a woman who can't bring a dowry?'

It was that night that Shanbagam did remember to ask Kumaresu. 'Do you want a boy or a girl?'

He laughed. 'What a foolish question!' he said, just as she had expected.

'It is certainly foolish,' she agreed. 'It was Janakiakka who made me ask you. She said you'd say you wanted only a son.'

'Can there be any doubt about it?'

She looked at him, taken aback. 'Giving birth to a boy or a girl is not in my hands, is it?'

'You ought to be clever enough and see to it that you don't have a girl.'

'But how? What can I do if I happen to give birth to a girl?'

He pouted.

'Why can't one have a girl?'

'Now. That's what's called a foolish question. Just lie down.' She thought she would ask him for an explanation some other time.

She must comfort him. She must tell him, 'Don't worry that what has befallen Rangamani might befall our daughter. We can give her an education. An education that will qualify her for a big job. And then she won't feel the lack of anything whatsoever. She needn't give any dowry or donation to any man. She would look after herself. That is how our daughter is going to be.'

Rangamani was between sleep and wakefulness. A hundred thousand children were sitting on her breast. And they danced—*Dhom! Dhom!*—like a hundred Krishnas dancing on the serpent Kaliya.

Rangamani was choking. Terror parched her throat. She didn't know how to answer their question: 'Are you male or female?' 'I am Rangamani. Maybe I'm male. Maybe female. Am I a neuter? Maybe.' 'No, you are none of these. You are Kaliya, Kamsa, Puthana.' They jumped up and down—*Dhom! Dhom!*—and broke her chest open. 'Come on, jump all of you, jump. Kill me. Jump!'

Rangamani, Rangamani. When she slowly floated up and escaped from the unfathomable depths, there was no expanse of water. No Krishna. In her courtyard, now awash with the sharp rays of the sun, there stood a woman in a white sari. Rangamani awoke, sat up, rubbed her eyes and looked.

'Vanakkam, amma. I'm a health worker. My name is Mallika. I've come recently to this district.'

Rangamani gestured her to sit.

A girl from the city. Has had some education—her face proclaims it. She's new to this village. The one who was here before her was driven out by the people of the village. I know just what she has come here to ask me.

Mallika hesitated. 'It seems a child died last night as soon as it was born. Do you happen to know why?'

Rangamani opened out her hand as if to say that she had no idea.

'Are you a midwife?'

Rangamani shook her head vehemently to indicate that she was not.

Mallika bent her head and plunged into thought. After a while she spoke, stringing her words slowly.

'Look here. If anybody here does not want a girl child, let her give it to me. I'll pass it on to an orphanage and nobody need be any wiser. In case you don't want to do that, you can leave the baby in the cradle set up in the Health Center.'

Mallika stood up abruptly and left the place. Rangamani got up, went and rinsed her mouth, lay down again and closed her eyes. A cradle. A cradle for orphans. The children who had danced on her chest now clapped their hands rhythmically: 'We are orphans. We are orphans. Like you.' All of them whirled around and clapped. They gestured with their hands: 'Orphans, Orphans.' Tears flowed from Rangamani's eyes. She wanted to beat her breast and cry. 'My darlings, O my darlings.' Her hands felt bruised and torn and painful. She bit and mauled her hands like one possessed. She didn't like the idea of getting up. Nor that of eating. Time crawled.

'Rangamani, Rangamani.' No one, no one at all need call me. I just don't have any strength left.

'Rangamani, Rangamani.' When she opened her eyes after much effort, it was dark. Darkness everywhere. Perhaps this was hell.

'Rangamani, Rangamani.' Gradually, her senses woke up. She got up and opened the door. Janaki was standing outside holding a lantern. Behind her stood a man who wore a turban—her husband or brother-in-law.

'Kamakshi's pains have started, Rangamani. They asked me to fetch you.'

Silently, as if she was walking in her sleep, Rangamani picked up her black sheet, covered herself with it and set out. Her head reeled. She felt utterly drained out.

Shanbagam woke up all of a sudden. From the rear portion of the house came noises and the sound of people moving about. Kumaresu lay fast asleep beside her. She got up noiselessly. Lights were on in the rear quarters.

That Kamakshi had started her pains was evident from her screams. Why hadn't she been taken to the hospital? Shanbagam was too scared to ask anyone. Ensconced on a chair at the center of the courtyard adjacent to the veranda was her eldest brother-in-law. Upon seeing her, he said, 'You go and lie down. There are people to look after her.' Only then did she notice Rangamani.

When she came back to her bedroom and lay down, the feeble moans of Kamakshi gave her a churning feeling in the pit of her stomach. The night went on and on. She sank into slumber, not even aware that there was a power failure a little later.

Rangamani waited at the steps to the backyard. Today she was overcome by a weariness she had never known before. She felt furious. Why do these women sleep with their husbands? She felt furious with that husband of Kamakshi's who was sitting there with his legs crossed, right in the center of the courtyard. Rangamani recollected Kamakshi's cry of desperation at every childbirth: 'I must bear him child after child, year after year as long as I can. There's no other way, Rangamani. He would marry some other woman otherwise.'

'Thoo! Are you a man? A human being?' In her mind, Rangamani began to chop off the parts of his body, one by one. What has invested you with authority? This? This? Here, off with it. A single clean cut. The orphans shall be transformed into Goddess Kali. Cradles have now been provided for them. They are going to annihilate you all. You shall be turned to eunuchs, all of you.

'Rangamani, Rangamani.' She woke up with a start. Janaki stood there, a small torch in hand. 'There is no electricity,' she said. 'You too can come inside. This night will be a difficult delivery.'

Kamakshi had no strength left to moan or to press down. In the dim light of the lantern, her face looked cadaverous. When her eyes fell on Rangamani, she let out a scream of terror: 'Go away, Go away!' Flames leapt up in Rangamani's heart. 'You woman, if you have any self-respect, any sense of anger and shame, take it out on that husband of yours— he who sits there, keeping an eye on everything. If he were not there, I could take the baby to the Government cradle.'

'Rangamani, Rangamani, here, catch it,' said the midwife, in a flurry. 'Open both your hands and catch hold of it.' Into her palms fell the child, warm, covered with blood. It let out a piercing cry. Rangamani straightened up with a start. It was obvious to her hands. A male child.

This was the heir to that husband of Kamakshi's. To that male, who was sitting there in the middle of the courtyard, shaking his legs, just waiting to enforce his authority. This thing is a symbol of his victory.

The midwife announced ostentatiously. 'Distribute sugar to everyone, Janaki, a male child is born.' A frisson passed through the entire household. After washing the child with warm water, the midwife said, 'Rangamani, cover it with a cloth.'

Bereft of even the strength to sense the happiness, Kamakshi lay limp, like a torn plantain fibre.

Rangamani looked at the baby. She took out grains of paddy kept tucked in her sari at her waist and thrust them expertly up the baby's nostrils. After wrapping the baby snugly in cloth, she left the place.

The backyard was pitch dark. It would be quite some time before the sky lightens, she thought as she dissolved in the darkness.

Kamakshi's husband's men are still on a search for Rangamani.

Shanbagam, who gave birth to a girl, is bringing her up alone.

Original Tamil title: *Nanju*

Translated by: Gomathi Narayan

# The Mousetrap

Sheelu was amused and wanted to burst out laughing. She had just realized that the ladies she worked for in the multi-storey complex were utter cowards. Initially, she had been in awe of them. They with their short hair, trousers, English…they seemed like aliens to her. They would leave their houses in their own vehicles even before their men left for work. 'You must complete your work before I leave,' they would sternly order. It was anathema to her mother-in-law Kamala to disobey them. Sheelu had been awe-stricken by these super women.

She had earlier done small errands in the houses where her mother-in-law worked. These days, though, Kamala had asked Sheelu to handle these houses by herself. 'Madams' were always in a hurry. It was impossible to please them, even if she worked at her swiftest. Today, she had been delayed by the antics of the madam who lived in apartment 203.

Just thinking about it made her want to laugh. A couple of men in the lift looked at her strangely when she kept smiling unable to hide her mirth. She pretended not to notice them. Did one not have the freedom to even laugh?

She could smell Madam's perfume on her shoulder, accompanying her as she walked. She recalled the scared, made-up face she had witnessed. Sheelu had been working in the kitchen when madam had walked in to open a shelf. She had screamed and held on to Sheelu tightly in the next instant, her face buried in Sheelu's shoulder. Sheelu panicked for a moment. What had happened?

'Mouse, mouse!' screamed madam. 'It just scuttled off this way.'

The family had gathered when they heard the scream.

'How did a mouse get into the house?' shouted the master of the house, as if it was a massive humiliation. Everyone spoke about it as if it was an enormous violation. They assumed that there was a hole in the house somewhere and planned to block it.

'Did Sheelu leave the main door open?' someone asked.

Sheelu stood listening to their angry chatter peppered with English. She wondered why they were panicked by a mere mouse. Madam still seemed scared.

'Madam, I will bring a mousetrap. Don't be afraid,' Sheelu assured her.

'Will the mouse get caught?' asked madam in a suspicious voice.

Sheelu was amused. 'That's how we catch a mouse. You should see how funny a trapped mouse looks!'

Madam wrinkled her face. 'What is funny about that?' she asked. 'Bring the trap and set it up,' she continued. 'Don't forget to bring one!'

The lift opened into the fifth floor and Sheelu hurriedly pressed the doorbell of apartment 503. She was still smiling.

'Come in. Why are you so late? Work quickly. I need to go out,' scolded madam 503, as usual.

Sheelu laughed as she narrated the mouse drama and went to clean dishes.

'Oh no, was there a mouse in that house?' asked Madam in an anxious voice.

'What women are these,' Sheelu thought with disappointment. 'Why were they so scared of a tiny creature?'

The afternoon sun stung her head as she walked home after work. She spread her dupatta and wrapped it around her head. She was hungry. Snacks like aloo tikki and samosa were being sold by the roadside. She drooled at the smell of samosa being deep fried in oil but did not have a single coin to spend. Kamala made sure of that. Sheelu now needed to work in all the houses that Kamala had worked in previously. On salary day, Kamala would promptly appear to collect the money and leave. Sheelu had never asked for her share of the money. She consoled herself with the thought that she was working for their household expenses after all.

She heard a bell ringing somewhere. Someone had built a small shrine amidst the shops and placed a God's picture there. A picture of Jai Hanumanji carrying a mountain in his hand. He was a monkey. 'Everything is God to us,' she thought. 'Even a mouse.' A mouse is Ganeshji's vehicle, Kamala would say, and should not be killed. Maybe the madam with bobbed hair did not know that. A priest was offering prayers to the picture, swinging a small flame in a metal plate, ringing a bell with his hand. A few worshippers placed some coins on his plate.

Sheelu never gazed their way. She had been involved in the temple festival before she had left her village. She had loved painting her hands with henna along with her girlfriends during festivals, dancing and singing in the temple grounds. Oh, she had loved many things then. Like wearing bangles, anklets, singing…She had worshipped with the others but had never felt like asking God for anything. The temple seemed to exist for organizing festivals. Could there be a link between her and the God draped in shiny silks inside the temple?

If so, how tough for God. How could He handle so many humans? That is why He must have gone missing somewhere. 'Handle it yourself,' he must have thought. Handle a mouse or hunger or a husband who beats you or a stern mother-in-law…

She felt like laughing again. A street dog looked up at her as if provoked. There was a stone marker opposite it. Sheelu sat down on the marker and stroked the dog's back. It closed its eyes and wagged its tail. 'Well, nothing to do except laugh it off,' she told the dog. 'Who is there to hug me if I cry?'

She had been told that her mother had died at childbirth. She had been married off in a hurry to the first available man as soon as her father was diagnosed with a terminal disease. He had died a month later. The dog opened its eyes and licked her hand.

Her friend Rama had told her that dead people sometimes came back as ghosts. Her father had not even appeared in her dreams. What could she say to him even if he did? There was only one question that bothered her. 'Why did you die, father?'

She looked at the dog for a while. It seemed like it had a resemblance to her father.

'Sheelu!'

She got up with a start. Her mother-in-law's booming voice resonated across long distances. Perhaps it was her voice or perhaps it was Sheelu's imagination, but she felt like Kamala's voice was pursuing her. She walked home quickly without turning back. She needed to get home to light the stove and cook. He would be there promptly at one in the afternoon, even though he was useless and unable to earn a single coin.

'Have you finished cooking? No? Where the hell were you gallivanting?'

One day, she got up from near the stove as he was asking that question. She spread her arms and danced like she used to with her girlfriends. 'Yes, I was dancing like this. Look, I got hundred rupees for that!' She had laughed and shown him the knot at the end of her dupatta. He had delivered a stinging slap, grabbed the dupatta, and unknotted it. It was just a knot without any money inside it. She had knotted it to prevent her dupatta from flying away. She had laughed again. He had slapped her once more.

She walked to the stove without a tear in her eye, as if immune to his treatment. 'Why should I cry? What mistake have I committed?' she thought.

'Look, if you beat me there is no food for either of us. I am hungry,' she had said and calmly continued cooking. He skulked to a corner and sat down as if defeated. 'How could one be so useless and yet be a dictator at the same time,' she had wondered many times. He demonstrated his masculinity only to her. He was a mouse outside the house. 'Give me money. Don't you have money? Here, take that... And that. I will kill you one day,' he would threaten.

She would laugh. 'How will you get money if you kill me?' He would beat her again. She was convinced that he was not a human. In a way, that thought consoled her as well. How could she expect him to be humane when he was not a human?

When she got married, her girlfriends had teased her about his fair complexion. 'Hey, he looks like Salman Khan!'[1] they had said. She had looked at him furtively. He was good-looking but she had realized that it was a mirage in a single day. Madan, her husband, had stolen her jewels and disappeared the same day she had stepped into her mother-in-law's house. He returned after several days. Her father had died in the meantime. As if he had been afraid to even ask, 'How are you, Sheelu?'

Kamala never said a word against her son. 'My destiny,' she would say sometimes, slapping her forehead.

1 Salman Khan: a famous movie star of Hindi cinema.

'Slap your forehead. You never even knew how to bring up your son well. You never sent him to school, nor did you know who his circle was. After allowing him to do as he pleased, you now say it is your destiny,' Sheelu would tell the stove when she was cooking alone.

He was not just a drunk. He imbibed all kinds of substances. Drugs too. Whatever they were. Things would disappear from the house. He would not come home for long stretches. If he did, he would molest her at night and curl up in a corner of the house the next day. Unable to tolerate his nightly harassment, she would often sleep in the back verandah.

'I was told that he would be fine if he got married. It is you who does not know how to please him,' Sheelu's mother-in-law accused her routinely.

'Are you blaming me for your mistake? Aren't you ashamed to tell me this?' Sheelu had retorted to Kamala one day. 'Your son is an animal, not a human!'

Kamala had abused her loudly, attracting the attention of their neighbours. 'Get out if you don't wish to stay here!' she had shouted.

Sheelu had been enraged but had wanted to laugh too. 'Tell me, where should I go? Did I elope with your son? You fooled my father and brought me here. Didn't you say your son was angelic? He is Yama!'[2] Sheelu had felt a fiery enthusiasm as she spoke.

'Go, go away,' Kamala had kept groaning.

2 Yama: The Hindu God of Death.

'If I go, who will handle the housework of so many people? Can you do it by yourself? Or will your beautiful son earn for you?'

'Or will your drunk husband bring in money?' she had wanted to ask but bit her tongue. That was an open secret.

Kamala shut her mouth when she saw Sheelu laughing heartily. She would often hear Kamala complaining to their neighbour. 'If my son is worthless, my daughter-in-law is crazy.'

Sheelu was used to all that now but she could not tolerate hunger. She would cook swiftly, fill her stomach, and drink a big glass of water. This was her idea of heaven.

'Go, go away…'

Where would she go? She could not fathom why Kamala should say so.

'If you get another man, marry him and leave,' Kamala had told her one day, out of the blue.

Sheelu was stunned. How absurd. 'Another man? In which shop will he be sold?' she had asked, opening her eyes wide and laughing loudly.

She had felt like her mother-in-law was the crazy one. 'I will never leave this house even if you shove me out,' she vowed to herself. 'Why are you telling me to leave? I work for your sake. I don't ask for money. I do all the housework. Do you find me a burden?'

Kamala had lowered her head.

'Look here. I did not come here out of love. You were the one who brought me here. It is your duty to protect me.'

Kamala had not broached the topic again. Sheelu was blessed to never remember others' anger. After working the whole day, she only wanted to sleep in peace. If she filled her mind with unnecessary junk, even her sleep would get disturbed. Oh hell, let them say whatever they wanted to!

She finished cooking. Madan was absent today. Good. She finished eating by herself. Kamala was absent too. She usually got food to eat in the houses she worked in. Since Sheelu handled several of her houses now, Kamala was focused on finding new houses to work in. Both earned twenty thousand rupees a month, since the men were useless. Her father-in-law Kishore Lal would come in only at night. Drunk to his gills. She avoided him. Shouldn't Kamala be chasing them out instead of her?

'Go, go away!' It was funny to imagine Kamala chasing away her husband and son with a broom. Sheelu wanted to laugh.

She remembered to place the mousetrap in her bag before she left for work that evening. She felt light-hearted when she stepped outside. The world seemed like a colourful carousel. The marketplace was close to her heart. Everyone there—vegetable and fruit sellers, shopkeepers selling cloth, men, and women—would acknowledge her and smile.

'*Kaise ho*?' 'How are you?' they would ask, as if she was born anew every day. In truth, she did feel that all things appeared to don a fresh beauty with every new day. She would enthusiastically wave and smile in response.

'First class!' she would reply. That was English. She had learnt it from the madams she worked for.

The shops seemed to overflow with flowers and fruits today. Shiny *zari*[3] and mirrors seemed to abound. Like it was festival season. She walked with a light skip and entered the multi-storey complex she worked in.

Kamala was waiting for her there. 'Sheelu, I had forgotten that we need to fast for *Karva Chauth*[4] tomorrow. Let everyone know that you cannot come in to work tomorrow,' she said.

'Oh alright. I will,' said Sheelu and walked on.

She loved festivals. If she applied henna to her hands and feet tonight, her fingers, nails and feet would glow red tomorrow. She would need to dress well and fast until the moon rose. Miraculously, she would never feel hungry that day. It was a fast for husbands. She was amused when that thought arose. She had been fasting for five years but there had been no change. She did not expect it either. The festival was just fun to her.

Kamala would buy two henna cones from the market today, each costing ten rupees. The mother-in-law and daughter-in-law would apply it on their hands after they had finished dinner. It was a time when both were relaxed and happy…

Madam looked at the mousetrap in amazement. Sheelu put a piece of bread inside it and enacted how the mouse would get trapped. Even madam laughed.

---

3 *Zari*: Fine gold or silver thread work used to decorate South Asian clothing and fabrics.

4 *Karva Chauth*: A Hindu festival when married women, largely in northern India, fast from sunrise to moonrise for the longevity of their husbands.

'Let's see if it gets trapped tonight. You must take it away and kill it,' she said.

'No, ma'am. We should not kill mice,' said Sheelu, shaking her head. 'Ganeshji will punish us if we do.'

'You are crazy,' said madam. 'Take it away somewhere beyond the metro station so that it does not enter this house again.'

'Oh, I nearly forgot, ma'am. I will not be able to come to work tomorrow. We have the *Karva Chauth* fast tomorrow. Lay the trap for the day after.'

Madam looked at her in surprise. 'What! Do you even do all this for that husband of yours?'

'Yes, why not? I only have one husband, right?' Sheelu laughed with great mirth.

It was dark when she completed her work and headed back. Madan was at home, an unusual occurrence. Kamala had already heated up the food she had cooked that morning and had also made fresh rotis. Her father-in-law was absent, as always. Kamala kept aside some food for him. Kamala and Sheelu sat in the courtyard after the three had finished eating and applied henna to their hands and feet. Madan was already asleep. Sheelu took a mat and pillow to the back verandah to sleep.

The dog she had stroked this morning was lying down on the mud floor. It looked up at her and wagged its tail. She found it funny. Seemed like it was trying to create a bond between them because she had stroked it that morning. She remembered that she had thought it bore a resemblance to her dead father. Perhaps madam had been right. 'I must be crazy,' thought Sheelu as she lay down. She was asleep in a few seconds.

Her girlfriends appeared in her dreams. They were holding hands reddened with henna and dancing in the temple grounds. They asked her if she was going to fast for Salman Khan. 'Look at the mirror. Do you see the moon, or do you see Salman Khan?' they asked. She turned over in her sleep. She felt like someone was untying her *churidar*.[5]

She was awake in an instant. Her tongue slurred in fright. 'Who is it? Who…' Someone clamped an iron hand over her mouth. She struggled. The dog started barking and she heard someone running from inside the house. One iron hand entered her *kameez*[6] and squeezed her breast. The dog continued barking.

She did not know who had come running from inside the house. The hand that restrained her loosened suddenly. Kamala and Madan were standing in front of her with sticks in their hands. She had never seen Madan so furious. Both flogged the man mercilessly, taking turns.

'You scoundrel! You arrogant bastard! *Kameene, badmash*!'[7] screamed Madan as he thrashed the man.

She looked at the man in the moonlight that seeped through the trees. Her father-in-law lay on the ground with

---

5 *Churidar*: Tight-fitting trousers worn by both men and women in the Indian subcontinent.

6 *Kameez*: A loose long top worn over cloth trousers by both men and women in the Indian subcontinent.

7 *Kameene, badmash*: wretch; bad or evil man.

a gash on his head, blood spurting out of it. The dog had run away, scared. Sheelu opened her eyes wide in shock as she took in the scene. Kamala was panting and resembled the angry Goddess Kali.[8] Madan turned to go in, as if indicating that the deed was done.

'I'm going to the police,' he told Kamala.

'I'll go. You stay,' said Kamala.

'Don't be silly. You must stay. Sheelu is your responsibility.'

Kamala looked drained and defeated as she glanced at Sheelu who was sitting on the ground. She shook her hand ferociously to remove the dried henna. Her palm and nails were blood red.

This wasn't funny. Sheelu wanted to cry. Anguish rose from the pit of her stomach, curling up in great waves. Sheelu broke into an uncontrollable wail.

Original Tamil title: *Elippori*
Translated by: Sukanya Venkataraman

---

8 Kali: The Hindu Goddess of death and destroyer of evil.

# The Untold Story

There was no one in the lift, which was a good thing. She liked standing in solitude under its whirring fan, away from the gaze of others. The heat and humidity outside would vanish there. The entire cosmos would dissolve. It evoked a sense of freedom inside her for a while. The sad part was it lasted only a few seconds. The lift was speeding up to the ninth floor. She was itching to stop it. To press zero again and go back. Perhaps she should never have come but hadn't been able to help herself. Her instinct had shoved her by the neck, urging her to go. She could not share that the demons, which had been waiting to ambush her, had started chasing her. Fear gripped her underbelly. What a fool I am!

Fool…Fool...

*There was an important meeting at four o'clock today. The exact time when Hema and Balu returned from school. Her father would go in her place to the bus stop to bring them home. Sumathi became absorbed in her work, lulled by a sense of peace this routine arrangement instilled in her. She had never analyzed why she was closer to her father than she was to her working mother. Amma (mother) was always in a hurry. She was engaged in housework until she left for her office; then work. Cooking the night's dinner when she returned home. Amma was tired by nine in the evening. There would be no time to even talk to her. Appa (father) became her confidante. He would take her to the park every evening and tell her stories. She would laugh heartily when he dramatized stories from the* Panchatantra,[1] *gesturing with his hands and legs. She wanted to laugh even now at the memory. She felt Appa was a great actor.*

*There were many files on her desk. Appa was seated on top of them. She moved him aside with a smile.*

The lift stopped on the ninth floor and split its mouth. She hesitantly stepped out of it. She turned right, as she had been told to. She spied flat number 901. Her heart fluttered. She wondered if she should turn back. She had been rather anxious when she had seen the message in her mobile phone that morning. 'Come without delay. Or you will be sorry.'

Old memories came roaring forth like a storm, weighing her down. She could not comprehend if what she felt was humiliation, anger, or sorrow. An insidious feeling. A memory that suddenly emerged like a fiend amidst her routine life and rattled her. Was it possible to erase it? She collected herself, took a deep breath, and pressed the doorbell.

---

1 *Panchatantra*: An ancient Indian collection of short stories, each featuring animals and ending with a moral.

*'Have you reached office yet?' She wanted to laugh at Appa's text message. He dominated all spheres of her life. He had supported her far more than Amma when she had divorced Vasu who had started another relationship after fathering two children. Those had been turbulent times. She had been blissful in her ignorance, unaware of the cracks that were starting to appear in her marriage. She had been disbelieving for a second when she discovered his other liaison and had been unable to contain her anger. She had felt like she had been pushed off a cliff when she had least expected it and would never get over the shock.*

*She had been enraged when her mother said, 'Try talking to him, Sumathi.'*

*'I am not someone with such low self-esteem, Amma. How can I live with him from now on? I too have my education. My job. I will manage.'*

*Amma shut her mouth but Appa had consoled her immediately. 'We are there for you. Don't worry!'*

*She could never have returned to her normal routine if he had not been there. She responded to Appa's message with a smiley.*

The door opened immediately. Ramamurthy stood there with a bright smile. The fragrance of his aftershave wafted beyond the doorway. She continued to stand outside.

He laughed and said, 'Come on in, come in. Why are you hesitating? Oh yes, you haven't come to this house earlier. This was purchased when I retired from my job. It has been a year since I moved here. Come on in.'

She looked around furtively and stepped in.

'There is no one at home,' he said laughing. 'Don't be afraid. The missus has gone to work. She will return only at six in the evening. After retiring, I opted to stay at home and relax. No more rush hours, no more clearing office files. I have a lot of time on my hands now.'

She lowered her head. She understood the meaning behind those words.

'What about the promise you made—didn't you say you would do it before you retire?' The question rose furiously and curled in, pressing down on her heart.

'Ah, I forgot to mention. I have informed my friends about your job. You will soon hear from them. Just wait and see.'

She looked up with a jerk. A spark hit the embers in her underbelly. She knew that every word of his would fan them into a conflagration. Still, she responded in a measured way. 'I don't need a job now, Sir.'

He looked at her in surprise, slight disappointment evident in his face. 'Why, did you get another job? Haven't I told you many times that I will get you a good job if you are patient?'

She responded in a measured way again, sparks flying inside her. 'Two years, Sir. How many times have you called me and tempted me by saying you'd soon get me a job?'

'Did you come to fight with me?'

She did not respond. 'Nothing would come of fighting,' she thought, sorrow constricting her throat. Whatever had been lost was lost. 'I did not come to fight. Tell me why you called me.'

*Sumathi pressed the buzzer after signing most of her files. Typist Sandya peeped in.*

*'Do you need to any letters to be typed, Madam?'*

*'Yes.'*

*In the meantime, she spoke to Rambabu who had come in to collect the files. 'There is a meeting at four o'clock. Check if there are water bottles and required things in the conference room.'*

*'Are you not going to fetch your children today?'*

*'No, I have already made arrangements,' she replied with a smile.*

*She became aware that Sandya was waiting and dictated the letters that needed to be typed.*

*It was an innocuous question surely. But suddenly she felt guilty, wondering if she was imposing too much on Appa. However, Appa was healthy. Further, he never complained. He did all household errands happily after retirement. Specifically, she never worried about her kids anymore. She would get them, if her work was done. If she was busy, Appa was prepared to do so. He would look after the children until she returned home from office. He would give them milk, make them do homework, send them out to play...*

*'Let him do it,' said Amma. 'He is sitting at home doing nothing.'*

*'Sweet of him' she said to herself.*

*What a relief it was that he was there. Her daughter was ten. Her son, eight. Her biggest fear was how she would protect and nurture them in a city where crime was increasing by the day. She could never permit them to walk home alone from the bus stop. It was dangerous to even have stay-at-home help these days...especially when there was a growing girl in the house.*

He laughed heartily. 'I felt like seeing you. And wanted to talk to you about your job too. Have you forgotten the past?'

'Didn't I tell you? I don't need a job anymore. I am married. My husband is a businessman. I assist him in his work.'

'Oh?' said Ramamurthy, looking at her keenly. 'No wonder you don't remember me nowadays. Earlier, you use to come running whenever I called you. Wherever I called you to!'

She lowered her head. The smell of his aftershave lotion wafted over to her. She felt like the intensity of her memories would make her tear up. She could see him shaking his feet rapidly through her lowered gaze. They moved right and left with an impatience that was familiar. She feared that those legs would lengthen and grab her like a hook. The figure in the chair kept growing. Like a demon.

'So, you are telling me that you won't come to me now, right? You cannot forget the past so easily, my dear girl!'

'Forget, I must,' she said with finality. 'I did not know the world then. I had come to the city from a small town. My mother worked as housemaid to educate me.' She could hear her racing heart palpitating. 'Do you know what poverty is, Sir? Do you know the dreams of mothers, Sir? And the anxiety of a daughter, looking for a job? She wants to give her mother some rest. She desires to educate her younger brother. She believes that all this is possible if she goes to the city and lands here.'

Ramamurthy watched her with interest, shaking his legs as she spoke without pause, pouring out the words she had memorized or rehearsed.

'When she is desperate for a job, a respectable man in a government job talks to her kindly like one concerned and tells her not to worry and assures her that he will get her a job. What will she, a small town girl do? Would she believe him or not?'

Ramamurthy laughed. 'Why bring up that story now? I have not forgotten my promise. I will surely get you a job. It will take some time; that is all.' His legs were moving at a great speed now. 'You came here knowing full well that nothing comes for free, right?'

She felt choked with anger that blazed through every part of her being. 'Do you know what desperation is, Sir? Driven to utter despair! You will never understand what it is to compromise when there is no other way. At that point, nothing was bigger than a hungry stomach. My mother's struggle was bigger. My younger brother's education was bigger.' She panted. She was afraid that she might cry.

He rose suddenly. 'Look here. Don't spoil my mood by talking nonsense. I have made tea. First have tea and snacks.'

She was amazed at how this man could speak in this manner. 'I don't want anything, Sir. I had my lunch before I left home.'

'Ah, well then. At least a cup of tea.' He poured two cups of tea from a flask on the table even as he was speaking. 'I can't help saying that you look better than you did before. Marriage seems to suit you.'

She pretended that she had not heard him and responded. 'You called me saying that I would regret it later if I did not come today. You said something about Twitter, Facebook. I could not understand anything.'

*Sandya knocked on the door as she entered. 'Your lunch has arrived, Madam,' she said as she brought in a tiffin set. She placed it on a table in one corner of the room and left.*

*It seemed that her father had consumed her whole life, when she realized that this too was his doing—organizing her lunch to be delivered. At times she felt embarrassed, wondering if Amma felt that his attention was unnatural.*

*He had retired from an honourable and prestigious government job. He had vacated the house provided by the government and had started living in a flat in the street next to hers. Amma had five more years before she retired from work. His being at home was a big help to Amma too. Sometimes he even cooked. He accepted buying fruits, vegetables, and groceries for the house as a natural part of his life. He would heat his lunch in the microwave and eat it. However, it seemed like Amma did not think that these were laudable qualities. In truth, Amma had never shared any opinion on this. She could not understand her mother.*

'Ah, now you are talking sense. Let's make a deal between us. Come over every Wednesday like you did today. Stay here for one hour and go. Like we used to meet earlier?'

She got up briskly and turned towards the door as she said 'Sorry Sir. I can't do it. I'm a married woman. My husband is a very good man. Besides, I am not in need of a job now. You can inform your friends not to bother.'

Ramamurthy leapt forward and made her sit by pressing down her shoulder with his hand. 'Oh, you cannot escape that easily. I have videos of all the time you spent with me. There, look at that small pen drive. It is all there stored. Just say no and it will be on Facebook and Twitter tomorrow. My face will not be seen in those videos.'

She was startled. There was a pen drive on the table. She went over to take it. He violently thrust aside her hand. Her body shivered with fright and anger.

'Would you feel good doing such a thing Sir? You don't want me to be happy after all the struggle I have been through? Please let me go. Please don't mess up my life.'

'Look here. I don't want to hear all that crap. I am calling you for just one day a week. Come like a good girl and go. You will not face any problem.'

*At two o'clock, she learnt that the meeting had been cancelled. Oh, she needed to let Appa know that he need not go to the bus stand, she thought. But this was the time he took his afternoon nap. She sent a message to his mobile phone. 'The meeting has been cancelled. I will fetch the kids. You need not go.'*

She sat quietly for some time. It seemed like the pen drive was growing exponentially, like a monster. It aimed at her heart. Her dreams shattered into a hundred pieces.

'Come, come. Don't waste my time. You are a good girl. I know,' said Ramamurthy, beckoning her.

She could see the bedroom in his gesture. She could hear the buzz of the air-conditioner. 'It is cool in there,' he smiled, reading her thoughts.

She took the teacups deliberately and went to place them in the kitchen sink. 'I will be with you in a moment. I will come.'

She noticed Ramamurthy plugging the pen drive into the television set. 'Come, come. No need to wash the cups.'

'Coming.'

He was naked when she went into the bedroom after washing the cups. He looked at her standing naked too, and laughed. 'Good girl! Come, I am feeling cold. Warm me up!'

She went close to him with an expressionless face. 'You are in a great hurry like always, aren't you Sir?'

The air conditioner sounded like a torrential downpour.

He stood there, spreading his hands out to hug her. The lust in his eyes was familiar to her. She entered his naked chest like a goring bull, stabbing him ferociously with the knife hidden in her hand. She stabbed him savagely as he started screaming in fright. Again and again on his neck, stomach and face. The stabs were deep as they followed the speed of her hand. She was happy that the knife was sharp. He staggered and slid down. His voice gone, his life silenced. Blood started flowing like a spring. She was stunned, wondering how she had been able to do this. She covered the body with a blanket, unable to contain her disgust when looking at it.

She went into the bathroom and cleaned the knife and her hands and legs thoroughly. She closed the bedroom with the air conditioner buzzing inside and remembered to keep the knife in its place in the kitchen. She put on her clothes and took the pen drive and his mobile phone. She erased her number and his call record on the phone. She wiped the mobile phone well with his handkerchief, went back to the bedroom and placed it on the bed.

She exited the house and closed the door securely. Her mind was blank as she once again waited for the lift. There was, amazingly, not a trace of fear in her. The security guard was talking to someone in the complex entrance. He never noticed her. He had not checked her identity when she had come in either.

*She did not know if Appa had read her message. She dialed his number at three o'clock believing that he would have woken up by then. The phone rang for a long time. He did not pick up the call. Perhaps he had gone to the toilet. She tried again half an hour later. It kept ringing. She was slightly worried. 'What had happened? Would he have gone out without his phone? Had he fainted? In a flat, everyone lived their own lives, even if they only had a single wall between them,' she thought wearily. Besides, everyone went to work too. She tried to reach him several times by half-past three and failed. She called her mother.*

*'Nothing would have happened to him. He spoke to me at eleven in the morning. Maybe he has kept his mobile on mute. Don't worry,' said Amma.*

*Slightly relieved, she decided to go fetch her kids. Appa was not at the bus stop. She left them at home and hurriedly fed them tiffin and milk. 'Stay in the house. I will return in half an hour,' she said and started off.*

*She considered asking the security guard if Appa had gone out before entering the multi-storey complex in which he lived. She decided against it, swiftly went to the lift, and pressed the button. The ninth floor was deserted. She went to the entrance of 901 and opened the door with her duplicate key. The bedroom door was closed. Was he sleeping at this odd hour? She called him, knocking on the door. There was no response. The cold blast of the air conditioning blew into her face as soon as she opened the door. Appa was not in his bed. Would he have had a fall in the toilet? She moved forward, fearing the worst, then bent down startled.*

*Appa was on the floor. His lifeless body lay face up with a blanket over it. She removed the blanket, her eyes wide with panic. A naked body. The shock made her very breath stop and froze the sob that rose in her throat. His body was covered with stabs. Blood had flowed like a river and dried. The murder had been a brutal one. Appa must have tried to stop it. Why were there so many stabs? Why were there no clothes on the corpse? Was it a daylight robbery? Were these brutal stabs made for a mere robbery?*

*She stood paralyzed, unable to think.*

*Her voice shivered and sobs burst out by the time she informed her mother in garbled words.*

*'I am on my way,' said Amma.*

*In the meantime, she called the building security. She told them what had happened and berated their inefficiency in a loud voice.*

*'Who came to see him?'*

*They did not know.*

*'Check the visitor's register and tell me.'*

*There was no entry in the register.*

*'We only question suspicious characters, Madam. No such person came.'*

*'How useless were these people?' she thought angrily.*

*The security head and the society manager hurried in. The police came. The building security's CCTV camera had also failed. The police, in their turn, rebuked the society manager for their inefficiency.*

*Amma walked in as if in a dream. Sumathi hugged her and wept uncontrollably.*

*'Who, who would have done this, Amma?'*

*The police asked them to check if something had been stolen. Mother and daughter checked the cupboard and Appa's purse with shivering fingers. Nothing had been stolen.*

*'Check his mobile so we know who he called last.'*

*'I've checked. He spoke to my mother last. That person must have entered without his knowledge.'*

*The police asked, 'Does he have any enemies?'*

*She looked at her mother. Amma was sitting on the floor, her mouth covered with her sari. She shook her head as if to indicate 'no'.*

*'Are you saying "no" or are you saying "I don't know?"'*

*Enraged, Sumathi intervened. 'Ask anyone about my father. He could not have had enemies. It may have been a case of mistaken identity. Only you should investigate.'*

*The police made several promises and left. The entire building had congregated. People living in adjoining buildings peeped in too. Her entire office came by to express their condolences. She cried in front of the TV camera, unable to restrain herself. 'If this is the case for a retired senior citizen staying at home, then no one is protected,' she said.*

*She called the police often. They had not found any clues. 'This must have been someone with an old enmity,' they said. 'There could be an entire gang behind this. We will investigate who he was in touch with before he retired and find out,' said the police. Anxiety gripped her as they continued to talk. It seemed like they were talking about someone unknown to her.*

*Amma never speaks these days. She had not gone to the office for some time either. Sumathi hugged her mother with a sense of helplessness, as the latter got ready to start cooking. 'Why should such a good man face a death like this?' she asked.*

*After a long silence, Amma responded slowly. 'Sumathi, don't go to the police again,' she said. 'Perhaps it is good that we don't know who did this.'*

*'What are you saying, Amma? What an unjust death this is?'*

*'Listen to me. We do not need to know,' said Amma with finality.*

*'Are you saying that the criminal should escape?'*

*Amma did not respond. She started chopping vegetables in silence.*

*'This knife, why is it so sharp, Amma?'*

*'Yes, it is. Your father searched high and low before buying it, so that he could chop vegetables with ease.'*

*She could not fathom the expression on Amma's face. Almost a smile. Sphinx-like.*

Original Tamil title: *Appa sollaatha kathai*
Translated by: Sukanya Venkataraman

# Voice

Valli!...Valli...Valliii!

Her body quivered. She stood confused for a while. Did someone call her? She moved, her slender feet stepping noiselessly, not touching the earth, floating like dried leaves in the air.

'Who is there?'

'What kind of a walk is this, soundless, like a thief?'

A voice like thunder. A voice she was used to. That made her shudder.

Shudder with fright. A pervasive fright. Entering her veins, her breath. Making her frail body shiver and fill her eyes.

'Please leave me, oh no, leave me alone...I beg of you...'

'Chee, chee, useless woman...'

She could still hear someone calling her. She walked towards the sound, unable to figure out from where it came. She hurried like someone was chasing her. Her belly tugged and her breasts pricked. She took a deep breath and gathered herself. I must have lost my mind. But, how many rooms are there in this house? It was like walking through a labyrinth.

'Valli, where the hell has this girl disappeared?'

'Coming amma...' Her voice sounded feeble, caught in her windpipe.

'Where were you? I have been calling you for a long time. Clean this room fast. We have to go out.'

She nodded her head and ran to fetch the broom.

'She is such a dumb girl. But I don't feel like scolding her. She has a frightened look, like a startled hare!'

'She is from the village. She will get used to the place. Let her be.'

She did not hear anything they said. They spoke another language or their Tamil was different. She had no desire to listen to what they said either. She did her work briskly and followed their instructions. She filled a bucket with water, added a tablespoon of detergent that smelt good and mopped the marble floor with a rag dipped and rinsed in the frothy water.

'Over?'

'Yes amma.'

'Hey, is your voice always like this?'

She bent her head with a shy smile.

The mistress laughed. 'It is okay if you don't speak, it is enough if you do your job well.'

'I will.'

The mistress laughed. Valli did not understand why she laughed. Their laughter was as puzzling as their language. Not understanding increased her anxiety and created a scare, like being blindfolded.

'I have kept your *nashta* in the kitchen. Have it before you leave.'

She blinked. What was the mistress saying?

'O my god, I have kept some food in the kitchen for you to eat.'

'All right amma.'

'Valli, come here.'

'Yes, amma?' She cringed under the intense gaze of the mistress.

'What is all this on your neck? Did you get hurt?'

'Nothing amma.'

'Looks like a scar?'

'Nothing, it will go away.'

The mistress looked at her again, clearly not satisfied with her answer.

'Well then, go now.'

Her feet moved like breeze in search of the kitchen that was at the far end. There was something kept in a porcelain plate. Two chappatis and some vegetable. Her eyes filled as she ate. She felt like wailing aloud. Her belly too wailed. She managed to finish the food, drinking a large glass of water. She opened the tap at the utility balcony and washed her face. She wiped it dry with her upper cloth—Anjalai called it dupatta—and remembered to cover her neck with it, bringing the end of the cloth to cover her breasts.

It was a three-piece dress borrowed from Anjalai. She felt naked in this dress, as she was used to wearing a sari in the village.

'It is this dress that is comfortable to work in,' laughed Anjalai. 'It looks "super" on you,' she added. 'But remove the duppatta when you work as I do.'

'You do as you please. I need to cover my chest.'

Anjalai would laugh again.

As Valli came out the mistress was starting the car. Looking at Valli she said, 'Come tomorrow as you came today.'

'Yes amma.'

'Come, come…' Words like a mantra that had dragged her here. Now it seemed those words were ominous and frightened her.

'Come away, Valli. People will talk in the village, of course, but….Come away. Your life will change here.'

How? She could not understand. The tall buildings, the shining floors and glass windows belonged to another world. Another planet. How do I fit into this? What relationship will I have with these people?

Anjalai gets annoyed with her doubts. 'You work for the money they pay you. What other relationship do you want?' Then she mumbles, 'You still do not understand what you need.'

Valli crossed the road and sat on a bench near the place Anjalai had said she would meet her. The house where Anjalai worked was nearby.

The mid-morning sun was scorching. Shimoga was cooler. Both her breasts were heavy like they were made of stone. She folded her hands tight across her chest. She drew her knees to her chin and buried her face inside. She loosened the cloth covering her neck. My, my, why do the tears gush forth like an opened tap? It was not possible to stop the flow. Her face dug deep in the darkness…she could see faces…ghosts…dogs that lingered menacingly ready to tear you apart...to gorge you…voices…she brushed them aside and looked for something. It kept slipping from her hold…even the image became dim. It may even slip from her memory…. She wanted to lurch forward to hug, but could do nothing. Sobs rose from the pit of her stomach.

'Hey, Valli, why are you crying sitting here in the middle of the road?'

She did not move.

Anjalai's hand was on her shoulder. 'You do whatever you want in Shimoga. Not here in Bangalore. People will not like it. No one will even ask you why you cry.'

Valli wiped her eyes and looked up.

Anjalai appeared embarrassed and irritated. 'Tell me, what is the matter? Did that lady scold you?'

Valli shook her head then buried it in her folded knees, unable to face Anjalai.

'What then?'

'I will go back akka.'

'Why?'

'I feel I am doing something wrong.'

'Don't be stupid. You are doing nothing wrong. Come let's go. The sun has gone up. Sitting in the heat makes you more stupid.'

She followed her with her head bent. Akka will not understand my problem she thought. When they came to the main road, and waited for the speeding traffic to pass and then crossed the road, she held Anjalai's hand in fear.

Anjalai seemed to be deep in thought, which was comforting. She wished the entire universe was silent for a while. Voices had been filling her ears all the time. They chased her while crossing the road. It was a big challenge ignoring them. Perhaps she should plug her ears with a piece of cotton as Anjalai does because of ear ache. But Anjalai has something else too plugged to her ears connected to her mobile phone. She listens to film music all the time.

'Sweeping and mopping and doing dishes every day will make you go crazy,' she explains. 'Come listen to this!'

Valli placed the knob at the end of the wire in her ears. Yes, it was nice; made her smile.

Anjalai laughed. 'Doing house work is boring. But when you are an illiterate, what other job can you get? You cannot get farm work like you do in the village. There you will be among scores of other women working in the farm. Time will pass, though it is tough work. Here the work we do is lighter, but boring.'

'I do not understand the word "boring."'

'It means it is frustrating. That is when music comes as a relief. There is another 'matter' too—if the mistress shouts at you, you won't hear it!' Anjalai laughed heartily.

Valli too laughed. Anjalai used a lot of words she did not understand. Anjalai said they were English;

words she picked up from the mistresses for whom she worked.

'Akka, why do you have to work as a maid?'

Anjalai was silent for a few seconds. 'If I have some money of my own, I feel strong and free. Why should I depend on that man for my face powder and bangles?'

Not just that. She wears dresses in various designs—all suits that she calls churidar. All the house maids here dress well. Looks like they do the job just for this—to dress well.

'I told you, if you live here, your life will change.'

Valli could still not understand. Her dress had changed. But she didn't feel comfortable. Her legs intertwined when she walked. There was a constant fear lurking in her heart. She did not understand what kind of courage it was that made her leave Shimoga. No, it was not courage. Seated in a bus in the dead of the night, travelling stealthily like a thief shivering in fright and cold…it certainly was not courage.... She hugged Anjalai who was at the bus terminus in Bangalore and sobbed uncontrollably.

'Don't cry,' said Anjalai patting her back. 'There is no need to be afraid anymore.' Akka's husband was with her. She controlled herself and wiped her tears.

It was just a week ago. She was still not at ease with the wind in Bangalore.

'He is a good man.' Anjalai kept assuring her. 'He is always ready to help others. He readily agreed that I should get you here.'

How long will she be able to stay with them?

'A good man'. She did not know if there was such a man. She did not see him speaking much with akka nor raise his voice when he spoke. But he smoked most of the time. At night he came home drunk. Akka would cook for him and wait. Valli was not aware when he came home. Half of what akka cooked would remain in the dishes.

'He eats very little,' akka said.

'Then why do you cook so much?'

'Supposing I cook less, he would at once call his mother and complain that I don't feed him enough!'

Akka laughed as she said this. 'It is his drinking that is a problem. But poor man, he travels by bus nearly hundred kilometres everyday travelling to his work and back. Perhaps he needs to drink to get over the physical strain.'

It is a wonder that he does not beat her, let alone abuse her. Perhaps Anjalai forgave his drinking because of this. Everything about Anjalai was a puzzle to her. She wondered if she should believe all that Anjalai said of him.

'In the morning, when he leaves for his work he looks like a god with sandal paste on his forehead and a bright fresh face . By the time he comes back in the night the man completely changes. Like a man cursed...'

She knows Anjalai offers special prayers and penances to appease various gods hoping they would cure him of his 'curse'.

Anjalai surely loved her husband deeply. She would rush to the door as soon as she heard his knock. She would almost walk him by the shoulder towards the bathroom and give him a shower to clear his head. She even helped him wear his lungi and took him to have his dinner. Valli, lying on a mat outside in the terrace with the door closed and bolted firmly, could still hear the gentle movements of akka—cajoling him to eat, if he ate at all. She couldn't tell. She didn't know when they went to bed. There would be no sound at all. All the lights would be off and absolute silence would engulf the rooms beyond.

But then demons would come to chase her. Dogs would come to devour her, tear her apart. Dogs. On the face, neck, breasts, stomach, thighs—their sharp teeth gorging her flesh. She would freeze in fright and pain, unable to raise her voice. Her mouth would have been sealed under an iron palm. No, no, don't don't....There would arise a hundred iron palms to strike at her rolling head. There was a boulder over her. In the end, she would be crushed under its weight, breathless and torn to pieces...

Aaththaa, mother of mine, I can't, I can't....Take me away from this. We will go somewhere. To the woods. To the hills. Where there are no dogs. I will survive somehow. Or let me die.

There was the tiny sound of a cry. It entered her belly. It circled her intestines, invaded her vagina and burst out with a ferocity she could not contain. 'Aaththaa,' she cried, as her breasts pricked in pain. She rubbed them in a frenzy.

She wept silently. What will I do, I do not know what to do...

'How old were you Valli?'

'Aaththa said I was about 15.'

'Why was she in such a hurry?'

Valli did not answer. She had just started wearing half saree, *davani*.[1] Those were also days when she, along with Kamali, Shanbagam and Meenu, would bathe in the pond unaware of the fleeting time and then spend the afternoon playing *pallaanguzi*.[2] It was a time when she never dreamt that aaththa would bring an abrupt end to it.

'Let it be akka. I have come away from it, haven't I?'

'Then stop crying sitting in the middle of the road.'

'All right....Give me some cotton.'

'What?'

'Cotton. There is a constant noise that I hear.'

'Really?'

'Yes.'

'What kind of noise.'

'Let it be akka.'

Someone was banging the door. She woke up startled. There was bright sunlight all over.

'Open the door Valli! Are you still sleeping? My husband has left for work. Don't we have to leave?'

Valli hurriedly went to the bathroom and got ready.

'How could you sleep for so long?'

'It was a disturbed sleep. And bad dreams.'

'Just dreams? Forget it.'

---

1 *Davani*: A length of cloth draped around the upper body and tucked into a skirt at the waist. Part of the half-sari worn by young women in South India

2 *Pallaanguzi:* a game played with cowries

As they were leaving there was a man from Shimoga waiting for them. A sudden fear gripped Valli.

'What, what is the matter?' her voice was hardly audible drowned in the wave of fear that rose from her belly.

'You must come to Shimoga immediately. The little one is not well. I have been asked to take you back.'

'Who said that?'

'Your aaththa.'

'What happened?'

'The doctor couldn't say. But says it is pretty serious.'

'Aiyaiyyo!'

Valli sat on the floor and began to cry. 'I told you akka about the bad dream!'

'Don't worry. Leave now with this man. Come back when all is well.'

Valli hurriedly packed her clothes in a small bag.

'Come back when everything is okay.'

She felt like weeping. 'Let us see akka.'

Anjalai tried to say something but just said, 'Don't cry. Everything will be all right. God is there.'

Valli was not sure about that. She left without responding to it. She asked the man as the bus departed for Shimoga. 'What is the problem?'

'Vomitting and purging.'

'Very bad?'

'That is what they say.'

Tears flowed down her cheeks. She could not contain them.

'I made a very big mistake. I will never again go back to Bangalore.'

'You ran away listening to a brash city girl's words. Nothing unusual happened here. Hasn't the world seen it before?'

She did not answer. She felt teary again.

'Things will get well. God is there.'

Is He? She didn't know. She knew only to weep and bear silently all the blows she received. She never asked any god for help. She thought God must have more important work other than driving demons and dogs. She has gone to the temple along with aaththa when she was a little girl. Her childhood vanished soon. She forgot about god altogether. If there was indeed a god would all this happen?

Now she was desperate. She wanted to hold on to someone's feet and ask for mercy. All the way during the journey she prayed to a god who seemed beyond her reach. 'Please save me. I have sinned.'

When they reached Shimoga at last, she washed her face at the bus terminus and they rushed to the Government Hospital. It was scary to see patients lying all along the corridor. It seemed like they came there to die. At the far end of a large hall lay a tiny bundle on a cot. Aaththa had fallen asleep sitting next to it. When she shook her shoulder, aaththa opened her eyes, startled.

'Oh dear, you have arrived. Look what has happened because of your running away like a thief.'

Her eyes filling, she opened the tiny bundle with a pounding heart. Oh how thin she has become! She looked at the figure looking lifeless, her baby, Pappa, with no other name, eyes closed. She kept her finger near the nose.

'Not dead yet. Waiting for you to come,' said aaththa sounding merciless.

Valli broke down into uncontrollable sobs. 'It was you who asked me to go! Didn't you?'

Aaththa did not answer.

Valli could not control her anger that burst from within and spewed fire in words that she had long lost. 'It was you, it was you…did I ask, did I want….Did you believe what I said? Did you believe my words? Did you come to my help?'

She paused. Several heads from the neighbouring cots were peeping above the blankets. She bent her head defeated. There was a movement in the bundle. Like a flower blossoming the eyes opened and looked at her. There was a broad smile, like a miracle.

She became hysterical unbelieving. 'She smiles! She laughs! Pappa laughs!'

Something gushed out of her being. Her bodice became wet. She unbuttoned her upper garment, opened her bodice and took the little one and thrust her nipple into its tiny mouth. The mouth sucked at it with ravenous hunger. 'Sorry,' she wept. 'I kept you hungry.' She closed her eyes and mumbled, 'Suck all of it. Suck my breasts dry, a weight I bore for eight days.' All the pricks and pain dissolved with the touch of those petal-like lips. How amazing. She kissed her child's forehead and promised, 'I will never leave you again.'

'Where did the mother go leaving behind a breastfeeding child?'

She let aaththa handle the queries and sank into her thoughts.

'What does her man do?'

'Who knows? He disappeared soon after the child was born.'

'What a cad! She herself looks like a child?'

'Yes, my foolishness. When she was about to turn fifteen I thought it is better to hand her over to a man who will take care. I was wrong.'

'He will come back surely. Won't he?'

Shocked, Valli blinked and hugged Pappa close to her chest. She never thought of such a possibility. The very thought made her shudder.

The doctor who came on his rounds the next morning smiled as he said, 'You can go home now. Pappa is fine.'

'It is a miracle really,' said aaththa. 'God's miracle.'

When they reached home, there was a dog at the door. He came jumping towards Valli. She stepped back, afraid.

'Whose dog is this, aaththa?"

'You can say he is ours,' laughed aaththa. 'He landed here on the day you left. He stays here as if he came to guard the child and the house. He is harmless.'

She was not sure. 'He looks like a hunting dog?'

'Yes, he does look like one. But he does no harm to us. Don't be afraid. I give him only rice to eat twice a day.'

'I feel scared.'

'Don't be.'

'What do you call him?'

'Pichai.' Mercy. How strange.

She drew up her plans for the future that night, while lying in bed. 'Aaththa, I am willing to work in the farm. I will tie a cloth swing to a tree and we can lay the baby to sleep while we work in the fields. There may be some work available in the sugar factory too.'

'Yes, but the wages will be less than what you get in Bangalore.'

'I don't mind. We can survive here, however hard life is.'

They did get work at the sugar factory. Their job was to collect the molasses that came from raw sugar during the refining process and make balls of it. The dog too walked with them every day. They tied a swing out of an old sari to the branch of a huge tree and let Pappa lie asleep in it after her feeds. Pichai would stand guard. Valli thought it was funny. Pichai—God's mercy.

Anjalai called. 'When are you coming back?'

'I have decided to stay back, akka!'

'You are a fool. You will not get even a quarter of what you get here.'

'I know, but I cannot leave Pappa here and be there.'

Anjalai did not call her again.

Aaththa who was loading balls of molasses in the container came running. 'Valli, your husband is on his way here. People heard him say that he is coming to fetch you.'

She was too shocked to respond. Fear gripped her underbelly and her throat went dry. She involuntarily touched her neck.

Women around her clapped and cheered. 'Good times are ahead, dear girl. When he calls, go with him without making a fuss.'

'Whatever you may say, he is the kid's father, love for the child is natural.'

Love? That fellow didn't even want to see Pappa's face!

'What, Valli, won't you run to welcome your husband? You stand like a rock!'

'She would shiver at the sight of him!'

'Look, if you show your fear it will be his victory. You have to bring him round without revealing your weakness.'

How? What do these people know? She rose to her feet slowly. She saw him approach the tree as she glanced outside the workshop. He was advancing towards the swing. Pichai was nowhere to be seen. She froze with fear, but ran towards the tree like one possessed. He looked at her intently, while she leapt forward and picked up Pappa from the swing.

'Give me the child. I have come to take her,' he said authoritatively.

'Why?'

'Useless woman! How do you think you can take care of a girl child? She is to be discarded. The government hospital has a cradle for unwanted girl kids. I will deposit it there. I will then come to take you back.'

She looked at him terrified. He was coming near. 'I won't give her to you.'

'Don't you dare bitch!'

'I won't. I won't come with you either!'

'I am your husband, remember that you idiot!' He came to snatch the baby from her hands.

She shouted with all her might, her voice roaring across the land—'Pichai!'

She closed her eyes convinced there was no freedom for her from this brute. She heard him scream. When she opened her eyes, Pichai was all over him—as he swirled round, his dhoti slipping from his waist, he continued to swirl in his underwear, his thighs and legs exposed, his shirt torn, his naked neck that Pichai attacked relentlessly—blood oozing from his thighs, stomach and ah, the neck. Pichai's teeth digging deep as he kept screaming for life…

Valli ran with her child inside the workshop. Her whole body shook at the unexpected turn of events. She did not know what happened later. Pichai had gone.

People stood round him. They looked for the murderous animal all over. Valli could not contain her tears that kept streaming down her cheeks. While her mother and the others wondered and lamented about the gruesome attack, she was immersed in an inexplicable sense of gratification.

Anjalai called that night. Valli rushed to tell her. 'Akka, I didn't believe you when you said there was God. You are right. I really saw Him. He came as a dog.'

After a pause Anjalai said. 'You are an idiot. There is no God. It is a lie.'

What are you saying, akka?'

Valli could sense Anjalai crying at the other end. 'My husband has left me for another woman.'

'What?'

'Yes. I cannot believe that he would cheat me like this.'

Valli felt like laughing. She said, 'Akka come here. We can survive together, not be bothered by them anymore.'

'That is my thought too. I don't feel like staying here from now on.'

No demons or dogs chased Valli that night. She had a blissful, sound sleep.

Original Tamil title: *Kural*

Translated by: Sukanya Venkataraman

# He Came

Rehman was busy rummaging through his box looking for something. It was a small tin box where he kept his two old pants, two ragged full-sleeved shirts, underwear and vests—his sole possessions.

'What are you searching for?' asked Kishore.

Rehman looked up and tried to smile but that faded into a pout…'Checking if I can find some cash.'

Kishore inclined his head and said with a smile, 'I too searched my box and the pockets of my shorts. Found nothing.'

'How are we going to manage?'

'The Sikh temple nearby gives free food daily. We can manage our hunger for a while.'

Rehman nodded thoughtfully. He knew about the *langar* (community kitchen) in the gurudwara. 'Will they let me in?'

'Of course!'

Rehman was not sure. 'Let us go back to our village, Kishore.'

'Village? How? The train does not run now.'

'And so doesn't the bus. I know.'

'Then how will we go?'

'By foot.'

'What? Is it a joke? Do you know how far it is from here?'

'I know. We will somehow hold our breath and walk, Kishore. We can go back and die in our village. Better to die there than as an orphan here.'

Kishore looked at him, startled. 'How is it possible, Rehman?'

Rehman laughed. 'We must make it.'

Kishore shook his head disbelievingly. 'We are now in Mumbai. We need to walk thousand kilometers and more if we need to get back to our village.'

Suddenly, Rehman buried his head between his folded knees and began to cry.

Kishore, moving closer, hugged him. He felt his own eyes moistening. 'Don't cry, Rehman. I too wish to go back to the village. But how can we go? They have closed even the roads they say. Both of us came together. Let us manage to somehow get by here.'

'How? It has been ten days since we last worked. We have no money on hand. The company owner chased us away saying he can't give us any money. The government keeps telling us to stay inside the house. No one asks if we have money or food. The owner of this room will come banging at the door for rent. We are going to starve and die. Let us die amidst our people. I want to lie down in Ammi's lap and die,' Rehman wept, unable to control himself.

Kishore thought there was actually no comforting word to console him. Everything seemed to be going well until last month. Suddenly the government announced a full lockdown. Construction work stopped. Companies closed without any notice to employees. There was no one to answer thousands of anxious questions on when they would open again or when salaries would be disbursed. The police chased them away whenever they went and stood at the company's huge gates.

It was not just the gates of the company that were shut. Even the street shops had to close. Vendors who roamed the streets pushing their carts of fruit and snacks, were chased away. An inexplicable fear had been unleashed, a fear they could not understand. They were told that a poisonous virus had spread. It was in the air, in human breath, human touch. It was deadly and people were falling dead everywhere, all over the world. No more getting together at work, at places of worship, at food shops, hotels.... It spreads like fire, this venomous virus devouring men and women. Where did the dangerous virus come from?

They said all kinds of things. It seems that people travelling from other countries had brought it home. The ones who came on airplanes.

We have not come from abroad. We have never even seen how a plane looks inside. We do not have any disease. Why did we lose our jobs? They could not ask anyone. Just sit at home, they were told.

Rehman scrutinized the rice and wheat containers. There were some lentils and oil left. 'We can manage for four days,' he said.

'They will lift the full lockdown by then,' said Kishore hopefully.

'You said the same thing the other day and I believed you.'

'Did I know it would get prolonged? I don't understand what is happening.'

There was no television. They read frightening news on the mobile phone and it made them panic. It seemed like the outside world had moved away from them. Or they were thrown out of it. There was no word of hope from anywhere. Their neighbour in the adjacent room said they would never get their old jobs back. He had come from Bihar, just as they had come here from Uttar Pradesh. He suddenly disappeared one day. It was said that he had left for his hometown. How did he leave during this full lockdown?

Now Rehman says they should walk. It was bewildering even to think of it. Their village was close to Aligarh, more than a thousand kilometres from Mumbai.

Kishore was hungry. 'Come Rehman. Let's talk about this later. The gurudwara is nearby. This is the time for langar food. Come, let us go.'

'You go, Kishore. They will not allow me inside.'

'They will. I am sure. Come, I tell you.'

Rehman got up. He hid his skullcap in the pocket of his pants. 'I have to lie if they ask my name. May Allah forgive me,' he laughed.

The Gurudwara was crowded. An old man saw them standing hesitantly, showed them a place, and made them sit down. Hot food was served without questions. Rehman felt teary as he was eating.

'Hey, what is the matter?'

'I feel choked when I remember Ammi's words. Every day she would bless me that Allah will be with me wherever I go. Today Allah was with us,' said Rehman, wiping his tears.

'We can somehow manage if we get food like this every day,' said Kishore after they had eaten their fill and were leaving.

'Brother, this is the last *langar*,' someone said. 'The police have just informed us we cannot converge like this for another two weeks. No *langar* till then.'

Both curled up and lay down as soon as they reached their room. Kishore kept worrying about Rehman's suggestion of walking back home. It was ridiculous, even the thought of it. Besides they had not a paisa in their pocket. They needed at least a hundred rupees to buy food and water on the way if at all they ventured. Who would give them a loan now? The company owner had disappeared. They didn't even know where his house was. Lockdown that came without forewarning was a new terrifying experience. As if an insidious force had stopped the world from functioning. The police were standing at every entrance as if enforcing its order. 'Go! Stay inside!' they say, chasing people away.

How could such a terrible thing come about? Like a curse? But it seemed as if only those like him and Rehman who were thrown out to fend for themselves were the most cursed.

No one had fever in the locality where they lived. They were hungry but it seemed like they had no disease otherwise, thankfully. Still, it appears that this infectious disease has come from somewhere. An invisible disease unknown to mankind until now. 'There is no cure,' they said. How strange. Was it in villages too or just in Mumbai? 'No, no, it is all over the world. People are dying in clusters everywhere. In countries they have not heard of. It may come here too. You may be the next one to die.'

There was no need for the virus to kill you. Without a job, without money to buy food, it was death already.

'In a few days things will return to normal,' someone assured them. 'The company will open, and work will commence again.'

They were able to live with hope for ten days. Then came the lockdown extension. For two more weeks. It was then that fear clutched their heart. How do we escape from this?

Ramu, Raju and Tukaram from the next rooms came by that evening and sat down. 'We are planning to go back to our village.'

Rehman started and sat up. 'How?'

'We are walking back.'

They too were from Uttar Pradesh but from another village.

'It is a great distance. How will we walk?' asked Kishore.

'We will manage. Some truck or lorry will go by. They say that we will get a lift for at least half the way.'

'They will ask for money.'

'There will be some good people. If we are lucky, we can reach our destination.'

Rehman's eyes sparkled. 'I have been saying this to Kishore. He is afraid. We are going to die even if we remain here, won't we? If we get back to our village, we will at least have our relatives to take care of our corpses.'

'Shut up Rehman. This fellow has been talking about death from yesterday,' said Kishore. 'Even if we do start, don't we need at least a little money for food and water? It will take four or five days to reach.'

'Don't you worry. I shall lend you two hundred rupees. You may return it later—when we meet next,' said Tukaram. Rehman sprang up, hugged him, and wept. Kishore too was deeply moved. It was decided that the five of them would start before dawn the next day.

'I saw Allah again today,' said Rehman when they left.

'Your Allah will be with us,' said Kishore with a smile.

They packed their belongings in a small bag with renewed energy. Rehman kneaded the little wheat flour left in the container and dexterously made six chapattis from the dough. He scooped the remaining pickle from the bottle, smeared it on the chapattis and packed them. Kishore was amazed. The fact that they had not noticed the amount of flour until now seemed like a good start.

They left while it was still dark. They were lucky; there was no police in sight. The empty highway spread before them once they had left the narrow streets. It felt like freedom, but they couldn't say from what they had been freed. However, it did not appear like the beginning of the next battle when they started out surrounded by friends. It felt like they would somehow reach their village. After about an hour, when it was light, they could see rows and rows of people walking on the footpath. Rehman looked at them and smiled. 'Look how many are walking like us. Are they all fools?'

Kishore was overwhelmed with the image that unfolded. They looked as if they were running away from an unknown horror, unable to face it. As if someone was chasing them. They walked, men, women and children with small bundles on their heads. Some were on cycles.

'Kishore, remember, how we used to roam around the village on our cycles!' said Rehman.

'We will do that again when we reach the village. On my uncle's cycle.' Kishore smiled trying not to appear cynical. They had not even crossed the borders of Mumbai.

Rehman had started talking as if they had already reached their destination. Rehman is a dreamer. He makes Kishore dream too. They came to Mumbai together in search of jobs. They dreamed together. Even if the sky was beyond their reach, they got contracted labour. Three hundred rupees a day seemed like an unbelievable income. They could send money back home. Agricultural loans were slowly paid off. There was never a time when they were separate except when they were in their own homes. Rehman's house was in the next street. Their friendship started by playing together as four-year-old kids. Rehman's mother was Ammi to everyone.

Kishore could not get rid of a nagging worry. Rehman's enthusiasm seemed misplaced. How many days will we walk? Will the situation in the village be any better? This epidemic has not reached the rural interiors they said. This was brought in by wealthy people, spread in the city. That was the reason why the poor migrants fled and dared to walk back to their villages. There is a roof available there for shelter. One can share whatever there is to eat. What is comparable to one's own soil brother? Kishore nodded. What they said was true. It was safe to be among your own kith and kin—on your own soil.

They ran along with the others. It seemed like the cosmos beckoned them with outstretched hands when they crossed Mumbai's borders and started walking on the road that led to Aligarh.

When hungry, they sat on the roadside and ate their packed food carefully, stretching it to two days. They bought whatever food they got on the way with the money Tukaram had given them. They sat down by the side of the footpath when their legs ached. They slept there at night. It provided some consolation to see others doing the same. Some good souls gave them food at a road junction. Rehman always thanked Allah in such moments.

Those moments were few. The long highway was empty. Those who walked with them had separated along various paths. It became hard to even get drinking water. Rehman tired fast and appeared emaciated. 'When will we reach the village?' he kept mumbling. The road seemed to lengthen endlessly, even as they kept walking with soles aching with sores.

'A lorry is coming!' someone shouted.

Four or five people stood together and raised their hands, a request to the driver to stop. The lorry stopped.

The driver asked nothing. The five clambered in. 'We need to go to Aligarh,' Kishore said, as he got in.

'I cannot take you to your street and stop. Get in, you can get down somewhere close by.'

'We have no money!' said Rehman hesitantly.

'Hey, just get in. Don't waste my time.'

'Thank you, Kishanchandji,' Kishore said, seeing the name plate on the driver's shirt. Rehman touched his head showing his gratitude. Kishanchand nodded. There were many inside, but it was possible to sit somehow. Rehman murmured it was Allah's blessing.

There was absolute silence inside. No one was interested in anyone else. They sat with fixed stares, as if they had met death. Kishore and Rehman leaned on each other and slept with the movement of the vehicle. It was morning when they woke up. Kishore was shocked to realize that Rehman's body leaning on him was abnormally warm. Rehman's face looked like a corpse.

'Water, water,' he murmured. Kishore was worried. 'Does anyone have water?' he asked in a raised voice. Those sitting around sat in silence.

'We are not any better than you. Where will we have water, son?' said an old man.

The lorry stopped at a road crossing. The driver Kishanchand came by. 'We will stop here for 20 minutes. Somebody is supplying water and also something to eat. Go get it,' he told them.

Kishore made Rehman sit down and ran. They were volunteers, four or five young men. They were handing out two buns along with a water bottle to each. Accepting them an old man wept. 'We have become beggars, son!'

Kishore hurriedly made Rehman drink water. His body was boiling. Kishore panicked, wondering what this new test was. He could hardly eat the bun though he was hungry.

'Kishore, don't leave me.'

Kishore wanted to cry. 'No, never, Rehman.' He felt weak and defeated, unable to contain his tears.

Rehman had a frail body. 'What madness made us undertake this journey,' Kishore thought in panic. 'Can we reach our village?' He did not understand how much more they needed to travel. The lorry was rolling on. He was amazed at how the driver had appeared like an angel and was taking them there. That must be a sign for good things to come. But it was worrying that Rehman lay still without even a murmur, his eyes closed.

Suddenly those sitting next to them started talking. 'Seems like this boy is dead. You get down here, somewhere. How can we travel with a dead body?'

Fear and sorrow constricted Kishore's heart. 'Please don't say that. I request you with folded hands, Sir. Please think of him as your son. He has a fever. That's all.'

'Is he your brother?'

'He is like my brother.'

'Looks like a Muslim boy?'

'We grew up together.'

There was a change in their demeanour. 'It was wrong to let you get in with him,' said one.

'I should not open my mouth whatever they say,' Kishore thought. The driver was not listening to any of this, fortunately.

Someone shook him. The others sitting close by looked at him angrily when he opened his eyes. 'Look, your friend is dead.'

Kishore looked down, alarmed. Rehman was speechless, breathless, his eyes gazing upward. 'Rehman, Rehman,' said Kishore in panic and wept. 'He must have fainted. Please, someone give a little water.'

Noise erupted around him. They went to the driver's side and asked him to stop the lorry. The driver got down and came up to them. 'What is the matter?' he asked, irritated.

'This boy is dead. How can we sit with a corpse?'

'No, he is not dead!' Kishore wailed and wept. 'Brother Kishanchand, if there is a hospital somewhere, please leave us there.'

'This little boy thinks we are fools. Take a look yourself. It must be an hour since life left him.'

'He was blabbering 'Ammi, Ammi.'

'A Muslim boy too.'

'Let him leave the body here along the roadside and travel alone with us.'

'Oh my God, I will never leave him and go. I need to get him to his Ammi.'

The driver stared at him. 'Come to the front. The seat next to mine is empty. Lift your friend. Don't sit with these people.'

The others started talking in random. If only the police know, questioned one. 'Get down if you don't wish to go on,' admonished Kishanchand, the driver. They shut their mouths. Kishore sat on the front seat with Rehman on his lap, his mind in a daze. There were pictures of gods opposite him, including the Sikh guru and Jesus.

Kishanchand addressed him briefly. 'No need to get to a hospital now. Just go to your village.'

Is Rehman dead? What am I going to tell his Ammi?

He hailed every God that he remembered. Krishna, Ram Lala, Kannayya… Let Rehman somehow survive. The tears did not stop. Let some God save Rehman. Allah, Ram, come. Rehman used to say that he wanted to die in his Ammi's lap. Kishanchand continued to drive, pretending not to hear him. It was comforting in a way, when he continued to drive on in silence. 'We are approaching Aligarh,' he said. Kishore told him the name of his village. A village with just two streets. One Hindu. One Muslim. They lived together as one family.

They have reached the street. And there is Rehman's house. 'It is this one, this one.' Kishore felt very weary. 'What will I tell Ammi?' Kishanchand helped him get down. He lifted Rehman on his shoulder. His legs felt weak and he wondered how he could walk up to the house.

Kishanchand went into the house, said something, and came out. Rehman's Ammi came running.

The whole street congregated in an instant. Speechless, Kishore placed Rehman in her hands. 'Water, give him water,' he said.

'Hey Allah, what happened to my darling?' Ammi cried. She wailed, placing him on her lap. Someone gave water.

'Rehman, drink, drink. Open your eyes. Look at your Ammi,' begged Kishore. 'Look, we are back home.' He kept pouring water into Rehman's mouth and on his face in a frenzy.

Ammi's eyes looked wild with shock. 'Kishore, what happened to your friend? I used to bless him everyday that Allah will be with him. That was my prayer. Allah has forgotten, deserted my poor boy.' Her body shook with sobs that wrenched the air.

Kishore felt like crying. He remembered that he had failed to thank Kishanchand. He wanted to shake Rehman awake.

'Allah came with us, Ammi,' said Kishore. 'Rehman, tell Ammi He came.'

Original Tamil title: *Oru Payanaththin Mudivu*

Translated by: Sukanya Venkataraman

# The Line of Control

He was gasping. The tunnel seemed to roll out endlessly before him. And running wasn't easy at all. 'I am old indeed,' he despaired. But run, he must. The walls of the tunnel were belching fire. Was he going to be cooked alive here? Curiously enough, the ground beneath was wet and soft. He could see Kiran running in front of him. He wanted to cry out, '*Kahan bhaag rahe ho?* Don't my child, don't!' But the words get lost in the deafening cacophony that surrounds him—the roar of avalanches, the explosion of earthquakes, the piteous wail of all things living. Look at that silly girl rushing out like that in the midst of all this. 'But just think of the poor calf, father!' she says. And there is Tiger, barking away furiously as if there had been a burglary. And this silly daughter of mine! 'Don't go Kiran, don't!' His whole frame is shaking in panic. His tears mingle with the runnels of sweat trickling down his face.

Someone was caressing his cheek with soft, wet strokes. Jagat Singh woke up. The surrounding darkness confounded his senses. Tiger continued to lick his cheeks. He stroked the dog's back.

'Looks like I fell asleep,' Jagat Singh muttered, surprised that sleep was possible at all. His *kurta-pyjama* clung to his sweat-soaked body. The shaft of light and air that had entered his bunker stood sentinel at the entrance on the right. He listened carefully. Was there any sound up there? Tiger whimpered.

'Shall we get going?' Jagat Singh asked. As if waiting for the cue, Tiger ran up to the opening, climbed out and waited for him. Jagat Singh stuck his head out through the opening and looked up at the dazzling sky and the quiet earth beneath it. Not a soul stirred in the street beyond the house. He took a long breath from deep down till his navel, savouring the fresh air. Tiger whimpered again as if whispering some secret.

'Coming! *Aa rahaa hoon*!' cried Jagat Singh, climbing out. Tiger seldom barked these days. He had barked his last bark when Kiran ran out that day. Tiger's whole behaviour had changed so drastically since then. As if the animal had forgotten his canine nature. Even as he had changed. Or, may be, he had forgotten his former self.

Opening the back door of his house, Jagat Singh let himself in. Stepping down into the courtyard beside the kitchen, he took off his *pyjama-kurta* and began to bathe pouring mug after mug of water from the concrete tub. Then he dried himself, pulled a *lungi* from the clothes line and wound it round his waist. Tiger was lying down with his face across the threshold as if guarding the house. Jagat Singh went to the kitchen, lit the stove, put some *dal* (lentils) to cook, took out wheat flour from a tin, and kneaded it into a dough. A sense of futility assailed him, as it did every day. What had life come to! There was no bread available for Tiger. It had been so for the past six months. But that seemed to be the fate of all the villages along the Line of Control. All shops had been closed. The village of Kargil was nearly empty. Men, along with their beasts, had carried whatever they could and moved to the camp at Akhnoor. Never before had people fled like this, never.

He had heard from his father how, during the Partition, whole villages from Pakistan had walked towards the Indian border. His father himself had walked down from Karachi. But now people were fleeing from their own land. Wave upon wave, village after village, wondering whether Death would come riding over the land or leap at them from the sky. For three years now, his mother's constant lament had been: '*Arre*, we might as well have stayed back in Pakistan. We came over here in the belief that this was our own land. Look at us now, dying a daily death!'

'If death was in our destiny, die we shall, no matter where we are,' Kamaljit had said. 'Remember my aunt who stayed back in Pakistan at that time? Her family was wiped out in the firing from this side.'

The day before yesterday Jagat Singh had been sitting on the front parapet as if in a trance. Tiger too must have been in some kind of stupor, forgetting even his constant whine. Tractors passed by, with their trailers packed with men, women and their children along with their possessions. Women with babies at their breast. The old. The sick. Utensils and colour TVs. Cupboards and chairs, spades, axes, winnowing pans. It looked as if people too had become inanimate.

'Hey Jagat Singh! What are you going to do here? Come along!' yelled grand old Chaman Lal who lived in the house at the turn of the street. His voice shook with the violent motion of the tractor.

Jagat Singh snapped out of his stupor and gestured with his hand: 'No I am going to stay here.'

'For whose sake?' The question seemed to float down from the old man, but was drowned by the clangour of the tractor's wheels. Though he could not hear it, that must have been the question; for that was the question flung at him by everyone who had left: 'For whose sake?'

No reason why he should give an answer. Those who are fleeing are doing so because they have somebody to live for. May be a baby born yesterday. May be some one spared by death. He has nobody left to live for. But why should the others object to his staying on? They had all stood dumbstruck when farmer Ajit Singh had cried the other day, banging his head again and again on the earth: 'What if one's family is lost? A farmer still has a duty to protect his land, hasn't he?'

All the while people had stood by with no thought of even comforting him. As though they felt it would be good for him to cry himself out, as though in the belief that Mother Earth would understand his tears. But then, once a man left his land, somebody else was sure to appropriate it. An enemy, even one of us. The fields have now been planted with land mines by the army—presumably to destroy the enemy. But look who got killed!

Ram Lakhan and his son from across the street. As if driven by the ghost, the rest of his family fled to the Jammu camp. Jagat Singh still could not bring himself to depart, though he had no specific reason for staying on. He had an oppressive feeling of not being alone. It was quite possible, as his mother used to say, that those who die before their time wander as ghosts. As soon as the sun goes down, he hears voices. He even finds it enjoyable, anticipating them. His mother's voice could be among those he heard.

These were anguished voices—voices with the haunting question 'Why were we killed?'

It was somehow incumbent upon him to give a reply. Well, those birds flying up there, were they all ghosts by any chance? The chicken and ducks, cows and calves and goats, all of them seem to have become wandering ghosts. The very air had now become heavy with their presence.

The *dal* was cooked. He seasoned it with cumin seeds and red chillies fried in *ghee*. Then he started to roast the chapattis. As the aroma of ghee came drifting to Tiger, he got up in a silent motion and came to Jagat Singh.

'Here. No vegetables for you. Just plain pulses. Not even onions,' said Jagat Singh to Tiger, rather apologetically. Without the least hint of protest, Tiger began pushing his plate forward. Jagat Singh let the chapatti cool a bit, tore it into four pieces and dropped them on the plate. Tiger ate them in silence. 'When will the Tiger bark again?' Jagat Singh wondered. He had mock barked at Tiger several times, hoping to make the beast give tongue. But, no, Tiger would just let the barking dogs bark and quietly lie down with his eyes shut.

Serving himself some *dal* and chapati, Jagat Singh went and sat on the small *mooda* (low stool) on which Kamaljit used to sit. He began to eat, watching the open courtyard that skirted their kitchen. Suddenly the courtyard began to fill with people. Nirmal, Kishore and Chotu were running from pillar to pillar at unstoppable speed, bursting with uncontrollable laughter. And there, sitting on the string cot, legs extended in front of her, was old grandma, enjoying the pleasant warmth of the sun. She flared up, 'Hey you, *shaitans* (devils), can't you keep quiet for a moment?' The laughter and racing continued, unabated.

Jagat Singh watched them with fascination.

The old woman complained, 'It's all because of that mother of theirs spoiling them so. Never cares to control them.'

Kamaljit, 'the mother of theirs', now makes a stormy entry into the courtyard, with her upper cloth slipping to reveal heaving breasts; she runs after the little *shaitans* and raps them hard on their heads with her knuckles. The shock of that knock has Nirmal, Kishore and Chotu bursting into a howl.

At this, Kiran—who had been at the sewing machine—dashes to the scene. She goes and kneels by the children and hugs them. Kiran rolls her eyes in anger at her grandmother. 'Why *dadima*, haven't you ever been a child? Were you born an old woman?'

Jagat Singh feels like laughing.

'Hey you, girl, you must learn to bridle your tongue,' Grandma chides her.

'You are a girl standing on the threshold of marriage.'

'You bet I am. Look there, the bridegroom is coming in the *baraat* procession! You *dadima* ought to be ready for it and not sit around like this.'

The children and Kamaljit laugh, their tears and resentment all forgotten.

'Children will be children, *dadima*. Please don't get upset. After all, they won't be so for long, will they?' says Kiran.

There in the corner of the courtyard must have stood *Yama*, the God of Death, unseen by any of them.

Kiran seemed to fill Jagat Singh's visual field as if she was the sole occupant of the whole courtyard. 'That complexion of Kiran's! And that glow!' thought Jagat Singh, his heart swelling with pride. My daughter, a wonder created by me! Her laughter, her tenderness, her cleverness… *Waahe Guru*! She is no ordinary human, but a goddess descended upon earth.

'You are crazy to dote on her like this,' teases Kamaljit, 'a daughter is to be married off and sent away to another family. How will you ever bear with the parting?'

It was going to be tough, he conceded. Kiran it was, who was now managing the whole house, from the doorway to the backyard. Kiran it was, who understood every one's needs. The calf, the cow, Tiger, Nirmal, Chotu. They were all equal in her eyes. She had been sitting at the sewing machine for a long time now, stitching something. Gold-laced embroidery glittered on orange coloured silk. Beads of sweat covered her fair face bent over the work, as she turned the wheel with her hand. Strands of dangling hair spindled her earrings as they fluttered to and fro.

'Who are you stitching that dress for, my dear?' asks Jagat Singh.

'Sheer waste of effort,' frets the old woman in reply. 'It seems some girl is getting married and our girl is sewing a wedding gift for her.'

The whirr of the sewing machine stops. Kiran locks her hands above her head in a lazy stretch. Her fair hands are crisscrossed by blue veins. She looks at Jagat Singh laughing. 'It is not for "some girl". It is for Somnath Panditji's daughter, Paru, my close friend. Her wedding is next Monday. She doesn't know I am stitching this for her. How thrilled she will be when I give her this!'

Kiran sprang up and shook the *kameez* she had been making. The silk and gold thread shimmered like a shower of stars, catching the sunlight from the courtyard. Kiran pressed the dress to herself and laughed. 'How is that?' Even the old woman laughed a toothless laugh, nearly mesmerized by the dress.

And that was when they first heard the firing. Before they could comprehend what was happening, bits of shrapnel spluttered inside the courtyard, just where grandma and Kamaljit were sitting. Shocked by the wails of Nirmal, Chotu and Kishore, Jagat Singh looked at the cloud of smoke and screamed: Kishore! Chotu! Nirmal! Maa! Kamal! —calling them one by one.

Tiger barked incessantly. The explosions grew louder and louder. Kiran darted past him like an arrow, running towards the back door, the orange dress still clutched in one hand. Tiger's barking grew frenzied. Jagat Singh shouted in alarm, 'Don't go Kiran, don't! Where are you going? Kiran!'

'The calf will be killed, father. I have got to untie it and let it run away.'

'Don't go, please don't!'

Before he could rush to her and hold her back, she was gone, the silly girl. By the time Jagat Singh reached the doorway at the back, a bullet had already pierced the calf's forehead. Another shot whirred past and hit Kiran. A fountain of blood gushed out from the side of her neck. Her body sagged to the earth like a heap of clothes.

Somebody came and stood by him. Jagat Singh turned and found Tiger looking up at him. He realized with surprise that he was standing at the back doorway.

He walked back to the small *mooda*, picked up his plate and finished the rest of his meal. Then he washed the utensils and put them out to dry in the sun. Thereafter he lit a bidi that he took out from a cupboard and stepped out of the house. Tiger accompanied him.

Jagat Singh walked on smoking his bidi. Now there was no sound of raining bullets. But the very absence of sound triggered suspicion, for the ear had grown accustomed to the menacing din. Does not the crouching tiger spell danger? Like death that had come all so suddenly, the other day? Yama had come without warning and claimed six human lives, not to mention the calf, the cocks and ducks, etc.

'*Arre* Jaggu!'

Jagat Singh turned back to look. Somnath Pandit was returning from the temple after locking it up for the day. He wore a dhoti round his waist and had a yellow towel thrown over his shoulder. The towel had the words '*Ram Ram*' printed in red all over.

Jagat Singh pressed his palms together in greeting and said, 'Namaste Panditji'.

'So you are still here, are you?'

'Yes.'

Jagat Singh thought of the orange dress Kiran had made for the priest's daughter, Paru. 'Has Paru left?' he asked.

'I sent her immediately after the marriage function,' said the priest in a conspiratorial voice. 'It was all gone through with such fear and tension and haste. Thank our lucky stars, the son-in-law lives beyond Jammu. So they have no cause to suffer as we here, on this Line of Control, do.'

Jagat Singh kept watching his smoke rings in silence. Orange silk and gold lace shimmered like a shower of stars in front of him. He had heard farmer Ajit Singh say that lately, it was becoming impossible to stop Somnath, once he began to talk. Some demon seemed to possess the Pandit, he had said. The air was thick with demons anyway, thought Jagat Singh. Hardly surprising if one of them possess a human being. According to Ajit, Somnath even roams at night, rifle in hand.

Somnath continued talking, 'Line of Control! What a funny name to give to a place where there is constant and uncontrolled fighting all the time! Our family has been in charge of this temple for generations. Where else can we go? So I thought "Let at least my family survive" and sent them all away to Jammu camp.'

'When was that?'

'Two days ago. Lots of people left. You could have gone too.'

Jagat Singh bent his head. 'Why should I? I can't leave this soil.' Then he added, 'Or this air either.'

Somnath was pondering something seriously. 'True. You shouldn't go,' he said. 'It is your duty to kill at least half a dozen enemies.'

Jagat Singh looked up startled. Half a dozen…what sort of a tally was that, he wondered, but decided to keep quiet. So that was Somnath's estimation of the extent of Jagat Singh's loss. A look at Somnath's face made him shudder. A demon seemed certainly to have entered the man.

'Panditji, I don't know who my enemies are,' he said wearily.

Somnath glared at him. 'You must be out of your mind. Tell me, was he your friend, the fellow who wiped out your family?'

Jagat Singh looked down for a while in silence. The courtyard rose before his eyes. He could hear those terrible cries and soon all was engulfed by a cloud of smoke. As the smoke cleared, there, in front of him like a scene from a film, lay those mangled bodies. Also those pointed finger-length pieces of shrapnel scattered around the corners of the courtyard.

He looked up slowly and said: 'He could be a friend. He is not responsible for the firing.'

'No matter who the perpetrator of the crime, that fellow is your enemy,' said Somnath, tying up his long hair into a knot at the nape of his neck.

It was obvious what the Pandit was driving at. Of late there was a daily circulation of handbills throughout the village. The burden of the slogan filled Jagat Singh with growing horror: '*He is your enemy; His religion is your enemy.*' Somnath was merely parroting it.

'Our army has laid mines in our fields and our Ramlakhan got killed by them. Does that make our army our enemy?'

Somnath slapped himself on his head in frustration. 'That was an accident. What happened in your house was murder.'

'There is no difference between deaths,' said Jagat Singh. 'It's not for you and me to counter such shoot-outs. We are powerless in the face of an attack that has no form, no face.'

'Perish if you must. As for me, I don't want to be a spineless coward.'

'What do you plan to do?'

Somnath drew a deep breath. 'I may lose my life in the effort, but there will be no redemption for me unless I kill at least one enemy.'

'Panditji has surely gone mad,' thought Jagat Singh as he felt a chill run through his spine.

'People seeking such redemption are roaming the streets on the other side as well,' he wanted to retort but preferred to keep quiet. Somnath had only to stand on the border, looking for the enemy, to invite certain death. They chased even shadows to shoot at. A sudden worry crossed his mind. What if Somnath considered Salim Khan an 'enemy' just because he belonged to the enemy's religion? But that was absurd. Salim Khan lived four streets away in the firm belief that that bit of earth was his birthplace. In as much the same way Kamaljit's aunt chose to stay back on the other side of the border. Somnath does know all that. But he is in the grip of a demon these days.

'Panditji, we have nothing to do with this war.' But Somnath was out of earshot.

Worrying whether he should have gone over to warn Salim Khan, Jagat Singh lay awake tossing and turning for a long time before he finally fell asleep. When he woke with a start, it was to the sound of continuous firing.

Jagat Singh snatched up the torch beneath his pillow and ran towards the bunker where he found Tiger already waiting for him. He slid down into the bunker. Tiger followed suit. As the pounding of his heart subsided, Jagat Singh sensed the presence of someone else in the shelter. Faltering a bit, he turned on the flashlight. A little boy! Jagat Singh felt a sudden sinking in the pit of his stomach. Was it Chotu? Tiger wagged his tail and licked the boy, who started to cry in fear. Jagat Singh chided Tiger, pulling him back.

'Who are you, little one?'

The boy began to sob without answering him. His posture, the way he sobbed, all reminded Jagat Singh of Chotu. To his tear-blinded eyes the boy looked like Kishore and even like Nirmal.

'Don't be afraid, my child,' said Jagat Singh. 'What is your name?'

'Akbar.'

That gave him a jolt. 'Salim Khan's son?'

'Yes,' nodded the boy.

It was pointless asking him what happened to his parents or his house. But the thought of Somnath Pandit did cross his mind. Surprising, Jagat Singh thought that the boy should have sought shelter in this bunker.

When Jagat Singh woke up in the morning, the day had an old familiar feel to it. In his arms was a boy sleeping. What had woken him, however, was something else. *It was the sound of tiger barking*! An excited full-throated barking. He woke Akbar up, washed his face and gave him breakfast. Then he saw a tractor coming in the distance. Must be *another* family fleeing bag and baggage towards a refugee camp.

Jagat Singh swung into action. Stuffing a bag with a couple of sets of clothes and picking up his purse, he said, 'Come on Akbar'. The boy took his hand most naturally.

Tiger barked and stopped the tractor. When everyone had found a place to sit, Jagat Singh caught sight of Somnath Pandit seated in a corner and was taken aback. Unable to suppress his suspicions and the great anger they roused in him, he confronted the man,

'Why Panditji, did you find the enemy?'

Somnath looked shaken. 'Don't ask me anything, the sinner that I am.'

Jagat Singh exploded with rage. Coming closer, he grabbed Somnath by the shoulders shaking him in a mad frenzy. 'What did you do? Answer me! You must!'

Somnath's eyes welled up. 'I couldn't do anything. An army officer told us that an attack was imminent. I remembered that Salim Khan had not dug a trench in his house. He had been postponing it, the fool. The shelter in my house is vacant, so I went to call him. I should have run instead. By the time I reached his place, it was all over. I witnessed it with my own eyes, Jaggu, but couldn't do anything.' Somnath began to slap his face with both hands.

Jagat Singh's hands relaxed. He gave Somnath a reassuring pat on his back and returned to his seat, next to Akbar.

After a while, Somnath asked him in some confusion, 'Who is this boy?'

'Salim Khan's son. He had come to my bunker.'

Somnath stared in disbelief. 'So this little fellow alone has escaped, has he?' He laughed sheepishly. 'You see, I thought it was your son Chotu. My brain feels so addled, Jaggu. I must have lost my senses.'

Jagat Singh slowly lit his bidi and took a long puff at it.

'Not at all, Panditji. You have not lost your senses, thank God.'

Original Tamil title: *Ellaikkodu*
Translated by: Gomathi Narayanan

# Acknowledgements

Bringing out this collection of short stories written in Tamil over the years, now translated into English, gives me immense satisfaction. Translating stories that are quintessentially Tamil or any Indian language that tries to convey a culture, codes, beliefs and ways of life is a tricky job that requires a sensitive translator to bring out the myriad contours of the original.

I have been lucky to find Sukanya Venkataraman, almost a newcomer to translating fiction, who lives in Virginia, USA, and was excited to do the exacting work. I thank her for her diligence and enthusiasm, ever eager to hone her skills. Gomathi Narayanan who has translated three stories in this collection is an old veteran in the field with many translated works to her credit. She is a sensitive translator with a keen grasp of nuances. I cannot thank her enough.

I thank Nirmal Kanti Battacharjee for coming forward to publish this collection on behalf of Niyogi Books, under their imprint 'Thornbird'. Most importantly, I thank K.E. Priyamvada, for her meticulous editing and her very thoughtful suggestions for improvement. I am grateful to all of them.

—Vaasanthi